To His Just Deserts

On a summer evening in the Great Courtyard of the castle in Savonlinna in Eastern Finland, audience and cast awaited the start of the final performance of *Don Giovanni* during the annual Opera Festival in the town. Only the singer of the title role was unaccountably missing, but his unpopular understudy was more than ready to take over the part.

During the performance, backstage drama surpassed anything visible to the audience, thanks to the involvement of certain members of the cast in the escape of a reluctant defector from neighbouring Russia and the added tension this entailed. But by the end of the opera it was the understudy who had disappeared. Had he, like the character he portrayed, been dragged off by one of several persons who had cause to hate him, to what the opera calls 'his just deserts'?

ONA LOW

To His Just Deserts

A Story of Finland

COLLINS, 8 GRAFTON STREET, LONDON W1

William Collins Sons & Co. Ltd
London · Glasgow · Sydney · Auckland
Toronto · Johannesburg

My warmest thanks go to Mr Pertti Mutka,
Director of Tourism in the Savonlinna Tourist
Office, for the many hours he must have devoted to
reading and commenting on the Finnish background to this novel, and to Sheila Rodighiero of
Venice who read and criticized ideas, expression
and contents in general.

First published 1986
© Ona Low 1986

British Library Cataloguing in Publication Data

Low, Ona
    To his just deserts.—(Crime Club)
    I. Title
    823'.914[F]   PR6062.O87/

    ISBN 0 00 231999 3

Photoset in Linotron Baskerville by
Rowland Phototypesetting Ltd
Bury St Edmunds, Suffolk
Printed in Great Britain by
William Collins Sons & Co. Ltd, Glasgow

CONTENTS

Characters

In Life	*In Opera*
Peik Arvika	Don Giovanni
Eeva Ruuskanen (his wife)	Donna Anna
Andrei Pavlov	Director
Natasha (his wife)	
Risto Aho	Don Ottavio
Ilmari Karhu	The Commendatore
Kaarina Laufach	Donna Elvira
Raimo Metsälä	Masetto
Sylvi Keskinen	Zerlina
Eero Virèn	Leporello
Hannu Hietanen	billed as Don Giovanni
Dr Markku Turunen	
Dr Ritva Turunen (his wife)	
Iris Lawton (English teacher)	
Arvo Laurila (Detective-Superintendent)	

The action takes place mainly in Finland

OVERTURE

1. ACCIDENTAL ENCOUNTER

A two-day-long thaw had softened the three-metre-deep layer of snow which had covered the Lapland fells for the previous six months, so that the few skiers who had remained at the Pallastunturi Tourist Hotel after the Easter season had had hard work and little pleasure from venturing out under the heavy grey sky. For a short stretch the surface might hold, only to give way suddenly with a cracking roar, leaving them to extricate themselves, skis clamping them down, from a squelchy porridge that might cover hips as well as knees.

During the night, however, the wind had veered to north, bringing clear skies and a keen frost which glazed the wet surface to mirror hardness and smoothness. A trio of Texans, who had been studying in Helsinki what had been their parents' native language and had taken time off to practise newly-acquired skills, experimented cautiously in front of the hotel but after a few falls decided against the risk of spending the next few weeks with a limb in plaster.

Having practically learned to walk with their earliest skis attached to their feet, Finns were less easily deterred, though they set off in pairs and trios rather than alone. The exception was a girl whose scarlet anorak challenged blue eyes and straw-blonde hair escaping from under her hood. Unperturbed, she started down the gentle slope from the hotel, only to sit down precipitately, gaze round in shocked surprise and scrabble on varnished ice to get on her feet again.

She found she was being assisted with gentle firmness by

a tall saturnine stranger, only not quite a stranger: he had
been the centre of a boisterous group in the hotel lounge the
previous evening and even then had in some way been
recognizable. Black hair just visible, dark dominating eyes,
aquiline nose and a pointed chin framed by a close-cut
beard: she was convinced she had seen his face somewhere
before.

He placed her firmly on her skis facing the world beyond,
dusted her down and for a moment looked thoughtfully into
her eyes.

'English?' he speculated.

'Finnish,' she replied in the same language, assuming it
was his own.

'Surely not,' he continued in English, American rather
than British. 'You're far too attractive.' His deep, potentially
powerful voice was provocative.

'Meaning?' she countered coldly.

'Are you alone?'

'Does that matter?'

'It does to me. And to you, too, I should think, on a
surface like this. Come and join us anyhow. We're experts
at picking people up.'

'So I've already noticed.'

'I asked for that. But only exceptionally pretty girls.'

'Who are we?'

'Myself. Peik. A nice short name you maybe won't easily
forget. And that guy there putting on his skis. Always a slow
starter, my friend Risto. But you couldn't find a better
chaperone. Absolutely safe with girls. Unlike me.' His hand
tipped her chin up slightly and he scanned her face, nodding
approvingly. As Risto joined them, he gestured towards
him. 'Risto, meet—well, would you believe it, I must be
slipping. I haven't asked your name.'

'Eeva,' she said, and added in Finnish, '*Hei, Risto.*'

Ski gloves ruled out the normal Finnish handshake, but
Risto managed to compensate with a gentle inclination of

the head, only to raise his eyes again in startled appreciation. With a muttered '*Hei, Eeva*' he turned away, concerned in trying out the hazards of the surface.

'OK, let's be off,' said Peik. 'Which way?'

'Not far,' said Eva. 'I'm leaving by the afternoon bus.'

'So you're really here all alone. Incredible. What's your boyfriend thinking of, leaving a girl like you at the mercy of Lapland wolves?'

'My friends—' the sibilant given due emphasis—'left yesterday. They're working girls.'

'And you don't work?

'I don't clock in at eight o'clock in the morning.'

'Well, well. The mysterious Eve. Corrupter of innocent man. Let's get moving. I presume, by the way, you normally proceed in an upright and not a prone position? We'd prefer not to tow you behind us.'

'I said I was a Finn.'

'So you did. I'd almost forgotten. Born with skis attached to your little pink feet, with your chubby hands reaching for the sticks.'

'Hardly so precocious as I imagine you probably were. In fact, not before I was two.'

'Not so far to fall then. But no good-looking guy to help you up.'

'Don't worry. I've improved somewhat since then. And learned one or two things too.

He grinned at her, turned and swung a stick towards the top of the dazzling white fell, set against a pale blue sky but unpeopled today with brightly-coloured moving figures.

'*Andiamo!*' he yelled to the horizon, before looking back at her over his departing shoulder. 'Risto's half way there by now.'

A lifetime's skiing experience was surely needed to keep upright on this curving, angled contorted, brilliant mirror, dazzling through the goggles pulled over their eyes before starting. On impenetrable ice, ski-sticks were virtually useless and with unpredictable cracks and swellings and changes in texture, only a more or less instinctive ability to adjust automatically to surface, to control speed and anticipate almost invisible hazards could keep them from falling, not into softly-yielding powder but on to rock-hard ice. Embedded beneath the ice, the parallel furrows of earlier, less restricted skiers were sometimes visible and in places sheltered from the wind, the snow was still slightly mushy. But for the most part, this was a crystal universe with a million rainbow glints sparking from the transparency, visible only when one or other of the three paused to lift goggles.

Peik halted to take a gulp from a brandy flask after getting no response on offering it to his companions, and set off again towards the fell slope ahead, commenting 'First time I've skated on skis,' as he did so. Now they had adjusted to the movement, the pace quickened somewhat, though they never lost their sense of precarious fragility. The ground was sloping gently upward to the fell, glittering in fierce sunlight, and the low-built hotel was now only a smudge behind them. The few other skiers had disappeared on their separate ways, leaving the three of them, black, scarlet, blue and grey shapes propelled by flailing marionette limbs, moving doggedly across a white universe.

At the point where the ground started to rise more steeply, Peik stopped and turned to watch the others coming up with him. He nodded appreciatively at Eeva, her face pink from the cold and exertion and frowning slightly with concentration, though grinning triumphantly at him as she slowed cautiously to a stop. Again the flask was offered and refused, Peik grumbling condescendingly.

'You don't know when you're well off, girl. It's not everyone who can have a well-stocked St Bernard with her when she goes on a ski trip. It'll make you walk on air.'

'Just what I've been trying to avoid doing for the past twenty minutes. And how about Risto?' she added, as the black figure, who had had to stop briefly to adjust a ski, slid to a standstill.

'He should have brought his own. I make a point of looking after myself and leaving others to do the same. You, naturally, being the exception. And now we start to ascend, who knows, maybe to heaven. Excelsior!'

'Not on your life,' said Eeva.

'Far too dangerous,' said Risto simultaneously.

'Amateurs! Cowards!' Peik roared at them in contempt. 'I've been scanning that slope for the past five minutes and there are dozens of ways of approach.'

'From below perhaps they seem possible but not when you are on them.' Risto's English was far less fluent than Peik's. 'The sun shines direct on the slope and some snow is again soft. But there is much ice also. You will be mad to try.'

'Some day or other I must die,' Peik declared, with apparent relish, 'and a cold wet hell would be preferable to a hot one. It seems, alas, that I shall not have your charming company, *bella signorina.* So, I take my leave, though for a short while only.'

He raised one ski stick in salute, bowing slightly, and set off upwards, moving transversely across the slope, pausing occasionally to test a surface cautiously and gradually plodding and sliding with growing confidence as he gained height.

Some thirty metres up he turned round to look down at their anxious faces. 'See what the faint-hearted miss?' he shouted, 'I've long been a rising star.'

He waved a stick towards the summit and the sudden over-confident movement upset his balance; he fell backwards, scrabbled wildly with hands and broken skis to halt his slithering descent and finally rolled over and over downward, gathering speed as he did so, his sticks clattering with him. He ended up in a sprawled heap a few metres from them and they were at his side instantly. After a few tense seconds he opened his eyes and glared at them. He swore in Finnish, Swedish and English for twenty seconds without noticeably repeating himself before adding, 'And if anyone present says I told you so . . .' Nobody did.

Before any assistance or advice could be formulated, he attempted to raise himself on his elbows but as he moved one leg, fell back with a yell of pain, embarking again on a series of polyglot monosyllables, on this occasion however coming to a halt almost at once.

'I repeat myself. And there are ladies present. Your pardon, madam, but something is not as it should be with my right leg, though whether a sprain, snap or fracture I'll leave to the medical profession to decide. My back's on fire, I'm bruised from top to toe and my head's spinning, though that's probably the brandy. Which reminds me of its medicinal uses . . . How fortunate the flask is of metal,' he added, drawing it out of a bag attached to the belt under his anorak.

'Would you mind staying with him while I fetch help?' Risto had reverted to his own language.

'An excellent suggestion,' Peik interposed in English. 'I can't imagine one I like better. You will hold the patient's tiny frozen hand, won't you, Eeva. Why so astonished, my dear?'

'But you speak Finnish?'

'Understand it, rather. I would never so misuse my tongue as to speak it. Off with you, honest Risto, though I'd recommend extreme care. If you break a leg, what happens to me?'

Risto glanced at Eeva and after a concerned 'You're sure you'll be all right,' set off towards the hotel. A kind reliable person, thought Eeva, but how unsure of himself he is.

She turned to the patient, who was again struggling to raise himself, muttering explosively as he did so. With Eeva supporting his back, he was able without moving his right leg to get into a sitting position and she remained crouching there, her hands behind his shoulders. He shrugged her away, however.

'Stand where I can see you,' he said. 'You know, you never realize quite how cold ice is until you sit on it. We must improvise.' He drained the flask, removed the detachable anorak hood, wrapped it round the flask and then slipped it underneath him. 'Not ideal but I'll survive. Let us now discuss higher things. Tell me about yourself, Eeva.'

'You're the mystery man,' she said. 'Are you another of the Americans studying Finnish in Helsinki?'

'I'm Swedish.'

'Swedes don't understand Finnish.'

'They do if they were born in Finland. It's forced down their innocent throats from the time Father registers the fact of their birth.'

'So you're a Swedish-speaking Finn.'

'A Swede who for no fault of his own is classified as a Finnish citizen.'

'And your parents?'

'The same. And their great-great-grandparents too. We were directing the affairs of this backwater before the Finns ever emerged from their trees.'

'And there are still Swedish-speakers who are so old-fashioned and narrow-minded as that,' Eeva wondered. 'I thought they had died out a generation ago.'

'A nurse's first duty, Eeva, is to entertain her patient. Tell me please about yourself. Where do you go from here?'

'Straight back to England.'

'To England, indeed. You are au pair? Helping mother with the little ones? A nurse, perhaps, training in an English hospital?'

'I'm a student.'

'Of English?'

'Of music.'

'Of music? As I am too. There, I knew from the beginning we were twin souls.'

'But a student of music?' She bit back in time, 'Surely you're too old.'

'How we repeat each other! And how unkind to remind me by implication of my advancing years. I'm still only thirty-five, not quite old enough to be your father. And a musician remains a student for life, surely.'

'Do you compose, play, sing?'

In answer Peik took her left hand in his, removed her glove and laid the hand against his cheek, protecting it with his gloved one and, in a caressing, mocking, rich baritone, with his eyes challenging hers, started to sing:

> *La ci darem la mano,*
> *La mi dirsi di si.*
> *Vedi, non è lontano;*
> *Partiam, bene mio, da qui.*

Don Giovanni was inviting little country-girl Zerlina to become the next of the over two thousand on Leporello's list, but this particular Don Giovanni was far more amazed at the immediate response than any previous one could ever have been. Full of justifiable mistrust, it delighted the desolate Lapland icefield in a half-rejecting, half-enticing soprano, clear, beautifully trained and promising future richness and range:

> *Vorrei e non vorrei;*
> *Mi trema un poco il cor.*
> *Felice, e ver, sarei,*
> *Ma puo bularmi ancor.*

Delighted, he responded with his own solo repetition, at the end of which they both spoke at once in identical words: 'You're a singer, then!' and both burst out laughing.

'Now I know who you are. Of course. You're Peik Arvika himself. When I saw you yesterday evening I knew and I couldn't remember. You're singing Don Giovanni this summer at Glyndebourne. I've already got a ticket.'

'Have you indeed? And when do you complete your music studies?'

'I have already; that's why I'm here and leave this afternoon. There are still some exams.'

'And then?'

'Find some kind of job, if only that's possible. Chorus work somewhere: here, England, maybe Germany, but that's not easy. Or I could do some teacher-training though that doesn't appeal much.'

'No, Zerlina, you deserve better than that, much better. I wonder . . . I'll have to think about it. There's no ring on this third finger. Neither wedding nor engagement. So it must be a room-mate with a nine-to-five job, which is why he isn't here with you.'

'That's my business, surely.'

'Don't be so sure. You'll have to break it off when you find a job, Eeva.'

'That won't be difficult.'

'Or could you actually be a sweet old-fashioned Finnish girl—is it possible one still exists?—who believes in marriage, lifelong devotion to one imperfect man?'

'Why not?'

'Why not indeed? You haven't, I regret, shown any interest in my marital status.'

'I don't need to. It's hardly a secret.'

'And you disapprove, naturally. But limiting my attentions to one paragon, would that be fair to all the others?'

'The thousand and three, you mean?'

'Only in Spain, a country I haven't yet visited but really must.'

'How about the six hundred and forty in Italy, the two hundred and thirty-one in Germany?'

'And the others in France and Turkey: my memory for statistics doesn't quite equal yours, I'm afraid. I have no Leporello. But why should you be willing to limit your attentions to one faithless man?'

'Must he be faithless?'

'I'm afraid so. We're all spoilt children, you know, Eeva.'

'Children can grow up. They can even learn to wash dishes and have children of their own to care for.'

'Children of my own I draw the line at. But washing dishes with a beautiful girl at my side to dry them, that's got something. I must really think it over. I might even lose my interest in Spain and Turkey. Could that really be possible, do you think Eeva?'

'There's a motor-sledge in the distance,' said Eeva.

'The first girl I've met who doesn't even listen to me, not even when I'm practically proposing to her. But perhaps you prefer Risto.'

'Is Risto a singer too?'

'We met in Melbourne. They were trying out their first Finnish opera. He's not at all bad, you know: as he's only a tenor I can afford to say that. Restful to be with: utterly dull. He'd make you a better husband than I would, Eeva. He's fallen for you already, you know. I know the signs.'

'That wasn't a particularly big brandy flask. But with the sun and the cold and the shock of course . . .' Eeva spoke absently, intent on the approaching skidoo, which was making cautious progress towards them.

'The original ice-maiden herself. Eeva, what's your address in London? You will still be there in a month's time when I arrive, won't you?'

'*If* you arrive, surely?'

'I've got to even if it's on crutches and with a leg in plaster. Rehearsals start in May.' The ski-based sledge was skidding to a halt as Peik released Eeva's hand. 'Never mind about the address,' he continued. 'There can't be more than thirty or so music schools in London.' Two men from the skidoo were preparing the sledge they had been towing for its burden.

As Eeva waited, uncertain whether they would need help, he sighed deeply. 'Remember, Eeva, no dates for—let me see—the twenty-fourth of May,' he said and, as the stretcher approached, '*Arriverderci, carissima.*'

2. AURORA BOREALIS

The mid-morning bus from Rovaniemi, capital of Finnish Lapland, to Kilpisjärvi, on the far northern Finnish-Norwegian border, was more than usually crowded this Christmas Eve. Students from as far as Helsinki had loaded the luggage compartment below with cases, bags and strange-shaped parcels beside the elegant air luggage of a Swiss family, a neat travel bag with a Hungarian name on the label, rucksacks and bags stowed inside by a youngish British group and sundry other items of luggage of varying degrees of smartness.

Many of the Finnish students were travelling alone and for the most part they sat quietly gazing at the steamed-up, frost-coated windows in unfathomable Finnish meditation, occasionally exchanging two or three inaudible words with their neighbours. The British spent the first ten minutes keeping watch for the sign denoting the Arctic Circle, missed it, and then exchanged jokes, meaningless to others and often to themselves, before falling asleep. The neat middle-aged owner of the Hungarian name on the suitcase label, who was sitting in the front of the bus, extracted a Gauloise, hastily replaced it as he caught sight of the sign in front of him but still lost nothing of his obvious serene contentment. A small alert unmistakably English woman with glasses and untidy hair peered at the Finnish grammar she was holding while her lips moved soundlessly in apparent repetition of the fifteen case endings of the singular form of the Finnish noun. At the other side of the aisle a lean tall man of around the same age, with longish fair hair lifted his narrow slanting Tartar eyes from his Finnish nature review from time to time to watch her with amusement.

The bus plodded on through snowlit gloom, pausing occasionally for some ten minutes at a coffee-bar which, together with a smartly-modern bank and a self-service store, formed part of each of the widely-separated villages. Gradually it emptied of students and after some six or seven hours came to a final stop, where the driver turned round to growl at them some incomprehensible but clearly vital instructions, which the Tartar-eyed passenger freely interpreted in excellent English as 'If you're going to Hetta, you've got to change here for a bus leaving in twenty minutes.' He then reached for his own winter hat and heavy overcoat, in common with his remaining companions who tumbled out to claim baggage, lugging it into a corner of the coffee-bar, where they lined up for ham, cheese or egg and salted herring open sandwiches, weak beer, warm water with a tea-bag, or coffee diluted if desired with cream.

Seated alone at a table bearing two plastic roses, the middle-aged English woman set to work on her sandwich, staring at the juke-box in front of her, praying that nobody would feel drawn to sample it. To her surprise, she was joined by a probable Russian she hadn't even noticed until he had translated for them. But his gentle 'May I join you?', his warm friendly smile and his unusually exotic appearance, at least for a Finn, stirred her curiosity and she smiled back.

He sat down and sugared and stirred his coffee, surveying with benevolent amusement the slightly prim suspicion of him she revealed without realizing it. 'I noticed you're learning Finnish,' he said, having sipped the scalding black coffee. 'You must have very great courage. By the way, I'm Ilmari, Ilmari Karhu; that means "bear" but I'm a very tame one. And I think we're both on the way to the Hetta Hotel.'

An attractive voice, certainly, unusually deep, beautifully controlled, with definitely a Finnish accent, despite his Russian appearance.

'I'm Iris Lawton,' she responded, 'a very backward learner, I'm afraid. After four months in this country even a bus conductor can't understand me when I tell him the place I want to go to.'

'He understands but imagines he doesn't because he expects not to: you're obviously not Finnish. A matter of psychology: the eye deceiving the ear. I expect you've noticed that often someone else will then repeat what you've said and he gets it at once.'

She nodded and smiled. He swallowed the rest of his still near-boiling coffee and continued, 'Where are you living here in Finland?'

'In Savonlinna. I'm very lucky: it's so beautiful there.'

'A lot of people would say it's a very small town, especially in winter.'

'But the people are friendly and very kind. I teach English there, in a number of factories and banks, with groups in each other's homes and privately. And everybody without exception wants to make me feel at home.'

'People everywhere respond to the way other people behave towards them. We Finns feel at ease with friendly people. And Finns are interested in foreigners, perhaps because they don't meet too many. They're not always so friendly and kind among themselves.'

'This would be Utopia if they were. Where are you from?'

He grinned, opening wide and shutting his Tartar eyes as he did so. 'Myself or my ancestors, do you mean? This face of mine—I didn't order it. It gives even me a shock sometimes when I see it in a glass.'

'I'm sorry,' she said hastily, catching her breath. 'I just meant where do you live?'

'And yet,' he continued, ignoring her embarrassment, 'I'm rather proud of my Russian ancestors and curious too, as I know nothing at all about them. Were they Cossacks galloping over the steppes, Tartars swallowing their raw beefsteaks as they rode into battle, choirs of Volga boatmen —the most likely, maybe? I only know my Moscow father married my Finnish mother in Viipuri in what was then Finnish Karelia: he'd been brought there as a child by his parents during the Revolution. He served with the Finnish army during the two Winter Wars and then came to Finland with four hundred thousand other Karelians when Russia took over their home. My father took the Finnish name Karhu for "bear" almost as a joke, I think. I was born quite soon after and grew up bilingual: I was never really aware of whether I was speaking Finnish or Russian.'

'And where did you learn English?'

'At school and in England and the States. Until I was nearly thirty I was an opera singer and I travelled a lot. Have you been to the Opera Festival in Savonlinna?'

'Not yet. I only arrived in September. But next summer, of course. Every opera.'

'Then all being well, you'll see—and hear—me again then. How well do you know *Don Giovanni*?'

'Better than most—it's my favourite.'

'Look out for the Commendatore: murdered at the beginning, dragging the villain to hell at the end. That's me.'

Iris frowned slightly. 'But excuse me,' she said, 'didn't you say you were an opera singer only till you were thirty?'

Her last words were only just audible as a bus had pulled up noisily outside and there was a general movement in the café to fasten coats and a scramble to grab luggage from the heap in the corner.

'That's the end of this instalment,' said Ilmari, as he stood up. 'Leave your listener in suspense and she'll follow you around to hear the next. That's your case standing near the radiator, I think, and mine not far away.' He took both cases, waited for her to go ahead and followed her to the bus.

This was a sixteen-seater minibus with space for luggage at the back and it was already almost full when Iris climbed in. She found a seat with three Australian girls who were working their separate ways round Europe. For the rest of the journey they kept her entertained, shocked, amused, fascinated by accounts of their individual hair-raising experiences, so their arrival at the hotel came as almost a disappointment. They swept her and her luggage, which one of them scooped up as if it were a feather, into the cheerful cosy reception lounge and made her promise to join them at dinner: they wanted the lowdown on life in Finland. Fantasy must run quite wild, she realized: what on earth could she do with classes for respectable bank clerks and coffee conversation sessions with shy housewives?

Ilmari was waiting for her when she came down to dinner, immaculate in a grey suit, and she found herself trying to smooth out some of the creases in a carelessly-packed, rarely-worn dress, and wishing that her always undisciplined hair with its natural wave had been a little less intractable after the long journey. She was even a bit relieved to be able to apologize and explain the promise she had made to the Australians: he looked slightly reproachful but while greeting the three already at table, she noticed out of the corner of an eye that he had joined at the table opposite hers two of the English girls, who, it seemed, had been travelling alone and were welcoming him warmly. A brush of disappointment, a faint touch of jealousy even, was soon dispelled by more hair-raising reminiscences as they sipped glasses of glögi, warm spiced wine with raisins in it.

Rice porridge and stockfish, soaked when iron-hard for twenty-four hours before cooking, were both rejected in favour of fresh salmon followed by succulent ham with a Russian salad. Bookings from three English-speaking countries had resulted in the unusual inclusion of turkey on the menu: one of the chefs having had experience in a London hotel, it was prepared in the best traditions. Christmas pudding being unknown or unthinkable, the meal ended with a cream and chocolate soufflé and a Finnish cheese plate. And then came Father Christmas in reindeer-skin coat to distribute presents, followed by a choir of Lapp children who for half an hour had abandoned family parties for a much grander one to sing Christmas carols in their own tongue in front of the ceiling-high candlelit tree.

It was her turn to provide the lowdown on Finnish life but she was becoming increasingly unaware of her surroundings. She had spent the previous night sitting up in trains with an interval at about two o'clock in a hard-chaired waiting-room and on a polar-wind-swept platform when a connection had arrived half an hour late, delayed by blizzards in the south. And now the food, the wine and liqueur, the warmth, the just audible taped Christmas music was lulling her into unconsciousness so that the faces before her blurred and swayed. She apologized, got up as in a dream and floated in the direction of her room, undressing and sinking into bed without even cleaning her teeth.

With an early-morning call arrangement forgotten, she slept until shortly before eight, too late to join the group who were to be carried the two hundred metres to the church service in the minibus.

After breakfast one of the Australians waylaid her. Having decided that Christmas Day had to be spent at the farthest point from their own country it was possible to reach, they had managed, through the good offices of the hotel and at a sum which must practically have exhausted their combined reserves, to induce a hired-car driver to abandon a day with his family to take them at least as far as the frontier at Kilpisjärvi and perhaps to the Norwegian coastal town of Skibotn, not much farther on. Would she like to join them? Realizing there would be light enough to see at least something—she wasn't sure what apart from snow—Iris agreed. The urge for adventure, the unknown, which one day she suspected she would regret, overcame the desire for a lazy day.

On this occasion there was no cause for regret. The night had been humid enough for the bushes and low trees to deck themselves in frost, more beautiful in its frozen perfection than needles or summer leaves. The snow-blue glow gave mystery to the fells and increasingly high mountains as they approached the coast. The other side of the world from Australia and it seemed from the whole of the populated earth.

Having existed on packed lunches, they returned in the evening starving. This time Iris avoided wine with her meal but even so she felt unutterably drowsy when she sank into an armchair before the huge log-fire in the lounge, a fire-waterfall reflected from it against the three protective panes of the large window. Around her she could faintly hear voices in at least four different languages and as many varieties of English: somewhere quite near there was the faintest click of backgammon pieces being moved and set down, and surely not far off someone was playing a recorder. She was just drifting into sleep when she felt a hand on the top of her head, and a quiet deep voice was saying somewhere:

'The Ancient Mariner who can a tale unfold cannot choose but speak, never having finished the one he was telling yesterday. And he has to leave long before you'll be awake tomorrow morning.'

She opened her eyes half-startled, and looked up at Ilmari. 'But haven't you travelled an awful long way to go back so soon?' she exclaimed.

'Oh, I'm not actually going very far tomorrow,' he answered, 'but it'll be some time before I see you again. And we've put on a very special Christmas display for you tonight, the like of which you may never see again. I know you're very sleepy after the hundreds of miles I hear you've travelled today. But if you wrap yourself up into a cocoon, ears, chin, nose—breathing doesn't matter—I promise you'll wake up, eyes open more widely even than now.'

There was a magnetism about this man which Iris resisted automatically but she did as she was told, went off and reappeared with little of herself visible apart from spectacle-protected eyes and nostrils. 'Well, perhaps I exaggerated just a bit,' he commented, when he saw her. He consulted the thermometer on the outside wall. 'Only minus twenty, almost tropical for these parts.'

But Iris wasn't listening: her eyes were on the sky, or rather the blaze of shooting, flaring, radiating, pulsating light and colour where the sky should have been. She moved down the road, turning on him irritably when he started to follow so that he retreated silently. This was her universe: it could be his too if he liked, but she wasn't sharing hers with anyone. Solar atoms attracted by the earth's magnetic force to Polar regions: was that it? But in that case these streamers, rising, fading, renewing, throbbing as they flared and raced through the heavens were quite literally un-earthly, caught into the earth's atmosphere from elsewhere in the universe, silent and unattainable and of immeasurable power. Purity, radiance and a glimpse of the primal power that had created and might still be creating the universe itself.

Without realizing it, she was moving along the road, unaware of its crystal-hard ice-covering, of the biting cold, of the distant barking of dogs and the subdued voices of other spectactors. And gradually the impulses weakened, the eerie light faded and on a sudden instant, she was gazing out at a universe of frost-brilliant stars. For a while she waited, looking around in disappointment, and then Ilmari, who had been standing a short distance behind her, moved to her side.

'That's probably the end of tonight's performance,' he

said. 'Just as well. Standing there fascinated, you could easily have got frost-bitten without realizing it.'

It took her a few seconds to become aware he had been speaking and what he had said, and then, with no great interest, she asked, 'Is that really possible?'

'It happens rather too often to over-absorbed skiing spectators.'

'How utterly insignificant we all are,' she murmured, turning back to look at the starry sky as they moved in the direction of the hotel.

'Minus twenty isn't the ideal environment for such discussions,' he responded. 'Into the hotel with you for boiling hot coffee.'

'You drink yours much too hot,' she murmured, absent-mindedly recalling a half-forgotten impression. 'It's bad for you.'

He shook the arm he was holding. 'Mutual bullying has ended many a friendship: this time, for a change, it's starting one.'

They shed outer garments, ordered coffee and waited for it in a quiet corner of the now half-empty lounge.

It was good to be in the warmth and firelight again and as she relaxed in her chair, she found herself yawning. Ilmari put down the scalding coffee he was sipping and commented,

'In a few minutes you'll be as sleepy as you were before I dragged you out so I'll answer your question straightaway, even though you've forgotten what it was. I'm leaving early tomorrow to call on a fellow I met at a conference last year: he's invited me to stay for a few days in his home not far from Sodänkylä. He's a vet, and besides the thousand and one other things vets do, he specializes in diseases affecting reindeer.'

'I see,' said Iris.

'In other words, you've no idea what that has to do with anything. Ten years ago I started veterinary studies, in due time qualified and am now practising in a village north of Lahti.'

He paused and, when Iris said nothing, continued, 'You're asking why should I do such an extraordinary thing and I'm not sure that I really know the answer. I just felt rather strongly that singing wasn't enough: just entertaining people didn't satisfy me any more. I've always liked animals, better on occasion than some people. They may or may not have souls but at least they don't have complexes: they don't organize hate campaigns or imagine themselves masters of the universe. But I'm not making speeches. So here I am, a vet. And in three or four days' time I move on to Rovaniemi and in the main church sing the bass part in Handel's *Messiah*—though in Finnish, which might surprise you.'

'It might have surprised Handel too,' Iris commented.

'He'd have been delighted. With all its wonderful vowels, Finnish is even more musical than Italian.'

'Do you practise on your cows?' asked Iris, who was now feeling very sleepy as she sipped her lukewarm coffee, 'and do they appreciate it?'

'Sometimes, to both questions. An excellent way of keeping my voice in trim, besides lessons of course, and minor operatic roles like the Commendatore. More coffee: it's half cold but might keep you awake for a few more minutes. Winter and early spring are busy times for vets, especially as my partner likes to take three or four weeks off for sunbathing in the Canary Islands, with a million or so other Finns. But in March perhaps something can be arranged. You'll almost certainly know the Turunens, the two doctors. They're great enthusiasts for English and opera too.'

'Indeed I do. They've invited me several times to their home near Punkaharju.'

'They're old friends of mine, so some time in March I'll be coming to call on them and so will you: I'll see to that. And now that we've settled everything, I see my new

Hungarian friend Mr Kadar has just come in. I promised him a game of chess this evening.'

Jan Kadar came up to them, shook Ilmari's hand warmly, bowed formally to Iris when Ilmari introduced her and then explained, 'Monsieur Kadar has fled from the uproar of Paris and only here is he far enough away to find peace. For us Finns he's a rather remote relative with a language that's even more remotely connected.'

'Do you play chess, Miss Lawton?' Kadar asked politely, in heavily-accented English.

Her reply was what he had hoped for. 'The last time I ever played chess,' Iris told him, 'it was with an eight-year-old nephew and he beat me. Now I'm so sleepy I couldn't even lift a pawn. So I'll leave you to your game.'

'So you are awake for the riding in sledges with reindeers tomorrow morning on the lake,' Monsieur Kadar suggested.

'Indeed yes. I wouldn't miss it for worlds. Good night to you, Monsieur Kadar, and to you, Ilmari, au revoir and bon voyage.'

Kadar produced his pocket set, took her place and the first of several games began.

3. PLANNED DEPARTURE

The rain had given over by four in the afternoon, leaving the streets of Petroskoi a treacherous mush of near-freezing water sliding over the bulges and hollows of the grit-grey ice that had once been snow. The clouds withdrew to the eastern horizon where they banked solidly, leaving room for the sun to take full control.

With the sun in his eyes, Andrei Pavlov laid down the pencil with which he had been annotating a large score, brooded for some five minutes and then with forced determination closed the piano lid and made his way to the

kitchen where his wife Natasha was correcting students'
papers.

'Let's go for a walk,' he said abruptly.

Natasha looked up sharply. 'What, on a day like this?
Have you seen what it's like outside?'

'I'm dying for a breath of fresh air. I've been two whole
days indoors. Put your rubber overshoes on and we'll hold
each other up.'

They emerged from the six-storey apartment block, identical with some twenty others around. Children were taking
advantage of the long-delayed sunshine to slither and splash
and a few of their parents were already on their way to the
shops.

A tall, burly, slightly stooping man, Andrei stepped out
unhesitatingly, apparently unaware of conditions underfoot,
while Natasha, smaller and less confident, having refused
the offer of a stabilizing arm, plodded determinedly and
with fierce concentration behind. With the phalanx of
honeycombed boxes behind them, they faced the waste of
ice and water that fringed the lake. Here they had the choice
between a struggle to keep upright on the granite-hard ice
paths through the belt of trees bordering the lake, and
sinking ankle-deep into the soggy wetness covering the
untrodden paths elsewhere.

As if seeking to make up his mind, Andrei glanced around
him before setting off down a frozen path which led to a
dramatic war memorial.

'We'll sit here,' he decided, indicating one of a scattered
group of seats, glistening wet and unoccupied. Having used
the copy of *Pravda* he was carrying under his arm to wipe
the seat reasonably dry, he sat down, remarking as he did
so, 'We can talk undisturbed here.'

'No doubt about that,' his wife responded, examining
unlovingly surroundings empty even of birds, before taking
her place squeamishly beside him. 'But why not at home,
over a glass of tea? Haven't you had enough breaths of fresh

air and sufficient exercise by now without enjoying a week
in bed with pneumonia as a bonus?'

'Don't worry. What I've got to say shouldn't take more
than ten minutes, if you don't interrupt too much. Something for your ears alone, remember.'

'You know very well that, except in a few essential cases, I
don't pass on information about other people and I certainly
wouldn't about you.'

'That wasn't quite what I meant. But we'll come to that
later.'

'What is it, then? We'll soon be looking conspicuous
sitting here on a day like this.'

He again glanced round and then sat staring gloomily at
the unenchanting thin grey ice-covering of the lake.

Natasha watched him uneasily before she demanded,
'Why all these dramatics? Have you been behaving fool-
ishly? Are you in trouble?'

Anxiously she examined his unusually grave face. He
turned towards her and took her gloved hands in his.

'I leave for Finland at the end of next week, as you know.
And, thank God, they've granted me my visa, both for
Savonlinna and Stockholm.'

'Of course, why shouldn't they? Our government is delighted with the appreciation shown for your work in the
West.'

'Natasha, when I go this time, I'm not coming back.' He
paused as she stared at him speechless. 'I'm sorry to shock
you,' he went on, 'but it's only recently I found out for sure.
And you're coming with me.'

In his capacity of a distinguished operatic director, her
husband was often away travelling in his own and other
European countries and his barely-concealed independence
and even criticism had made her aware of a possibility
she had never dared to face. With the fact now starkly
confronting her, she turned to fight it.

'You mean you want me to leave my home and my

country to go and live in the West.' She spat the word out
with disgust. 'What have they done to you with their lies
and propaganda and materialism? So they can boast to the
credulous world that another fool has accepted their bribes
and deserted his own country. I've always known you were
gullible and weak, but I've been so afraid that I haven't
dared say anything because I was a coward, afraid it could
be true. Well, you can go and stay there and have your
luxury hotels and cars and women if you want, but I'm
staying here where I belong.'

Too angry for tears, she drew away from him into a pool
of icy water at the unwiped end of the seat, her hands
clenched on her knees. Andrei again glanced round furtively,
and then spoke quietly but urgently.

'Whatever you think and feel, please don't show it openly,'
he said. 'Smile, for heaven's sake, as if we've been joking
and move back here. Someone could be watching even now.'

'Watching? What idiocy!' she exclaimed, looking in her
turn round the near-Arctic desolation. Even so, there was a
slight uneasiness in her survey, and with anger and shock
still showing on her face she moved reluctantly back to her
husband's side.

She sensed in him not resistance but a weary detachment
that all her scolding would be unable to penetrate. With
long experience she softened her approach. 'I'm sorry,
Andrei,' she said reasonably, 'you know how I feel and,
well, you can't not know you've just pushed everything from
under me and . . .' The tears were starting to flow and she
hid her face on his shoulder, before looking up at him
through enormous brown eyes to add, 'You always have a
reason for everything and I know you don't like the way
you say you're controlled here. But deciding to live over
there . . .'

'It isn't so bad as they tell you, you know.' He spoke
gently. 'Materialism, yes, but that exists in a more or less
advanced form in every country in the world and always

has: it just increases as more things become available. Decadence, yes indeed, a more obvious rat race, commercial exploitation; violence on the streets occasionally; you'll have been better informed about the evils theoretically than I am at first hand. But whenever I go back to Finland or any other country beyond, I feel the difference all round me: people walk differently, as if they've got somewhere to go and a purpose in living; they can make their own decisions, shape their own lives and careers, say what they think regardless of who may be listening and look ahead to where they're going and not around at who's watching.'

'And those who haven't got a job, poor people, sick people, old people? And the Third World?'

Hardly the place for a detailed survey of such wide-ranging issues. Andrei sighed, but before he could devise means of disposing of them satisfactorily in a single sentence, Natasha burst out:

'Can you deny capitalistic forces are in supreme control, that only the interests of the money-making classes, the multi-national combines and cartels, the avaricious industrialists matter, and to hell with the poor and helpless? Corrupt politicians playing for power, grasping business tycoons for money, a venal press for publicity, notoriety, and the middle classes out for themselves and their vanity and greed? They lie and cheat and build ever more weapons to use against humanity, against us, and to do this they exploit their own poor and bully and rob the underprivileged nations of the Third World. Where can you find our cooperation and discipline and concern for the masses, the proletariat? Where . . . ?'

It was at this point that Andrei lost the last of his self-control and let forth a bellow which ignored any observers there might have been, together with any illusions they might have had of the casual nature of the conversation.

'Woman,' he roared, 'stop mouthing propaganda at me as if I'd never in my life heard any of it before.' With each word the volume of his attack faded until he was addressing her in a reasonably controlled voice. 'Of course there's greed, deceit, selfishness, exploitation there as there is everywhere. I've admitted it: they're human beings just as we are. It exists here too, as you well know, only maybe more so because it's combined so often with stupidity and narrow-mindedness and petty despotism and uniformity. It's far too cold to continue being so childish so let's get to the point. We can resume the political background when you join me and can see for yourself.'

'I've already told you. I'm staying here—and you're staying with me.'

'In a gaol, a prison camp, a psychological ward, Siberia?'

'That's impossible. You're not a criminal or a dissenter.'

'I'm both, as they'd apply those words. And they know it.'

'Who are they? And what do they know?'

Andrei took her hand again, holding it this time between his own.

'Natasha,' he said rather sadly, 'you've never asked me much about my life when I'm away from you, have you? I know why, you know. You were afraid I was indeed being corrupted and you preferred not to know.'

'I was right to be.' She spoke bitterly.

'Maybe,' he admitted, 'though you might or might not have been reassured if you'd known that I wasn't alone: there was always a comrade close beside me. Our Embassy in Helsinki provided him for me to act as interpreter—though my Finnish was rather better than his and we use English in rehearsals—guide, adviser, and also watchdog, record-keeper, tape-recorder in all my local contacts, the shadow at my heels and at my shoulder. Just to make sure I wasn't corrupted, that I didn't get into trouble—from our Embassy's point of view, of course. And naturally I did.'

'What kind of trouble?'

'Knowing me, can't you guess? An evening in a restaurant

or someone's home: a few brandies or vodkas and plenty of Finns and other nationalities agog for the off-the-record opinions and experiences of the real live distinguished Soviet artist. And all the frustrations and bitterness I've had to keep quiet about here bursting the cork from the bottle.'

'What frustrations? You've had only privileges. If you had my life as a teacher—' Natasha braked hastily. 'You've just been praised and rewarded and spoilt.'

'My dear, if I'd tried telling you about my problems, you'd have just refused to believe me. But let's pass on. A local friend who shall be nameless—trees probably have ears here—warned me a short time ago that I was in for trouble soon, very real trouble, it seems. There was talk of cancelling my foreign travel visa but that wouldn't have looked good internationally. So they've said nothing to me yet, just waiting for my return when they'll have me where they want me. But I'll be watched every minute and, as I've been reminded before each departure, any Russian citizen defecting in Finland or arriving there illegally is automatically handed back. I've heard that contradicted by Finns but I'm not risking it. I know for sure political asylum is available in Sweden.'

Natasha's face was as grey as the clouds that were again building up behind them. 'So you'll be leaving Petroskoi for good,' she murmured tonelessly.

'Only if you're with me.' The tide was now in Andrei's favour and he was ready to take advantage of it.

'How can I? As if they'd let me go.'

'No, not with me. But there are other ways. There's a very long frontier with Finland that can't possibly be watched everywhere.'

'To walk across, I suppose. Can you really imagine me, Andrei, tramping through marsh and over barbed wire in the dark? And being sent back as soon as I reached Finland?'

'That I can't imagine, no,' he assured her. 'The subject has cropped up before in discussions with friends in Finland but until now I've never taken it seriously. But I'm sure there are safer and rather more comfortable possibilities. That's if only you're willing to try. After all, Natasha, you can serve your native country far better out of it than in.'

'I don't believe you. How?'

'The wife of the famous defector, Andrei Pavlov, the world-famous opera director, abandons her country for her husband's sake but finds that the West has nothing of value to offer. You'll be the idol of Communist parties everywhere.'

'Also in Finland?'

'Leave things to me. I'm quite sure something can be worked out.'

He lifted his head, listening, hastily extracted a diary from his pocket and started writing, with a finger on his lips:

'Don't look round. Somebody has just come up behind us. He's probably sitting down now. He might have long-distance listening equipment.'

He placed the message where she could see it without attracting attention, hunched his shoulders in a tremendous shiver and stood up.

'Enough fresh air for today, I think. I feel much better now. Shall we go and get some tea, my dear?'

They were careful not to look back until they were again among the children, shouting and screaming as they chased one another, and by that time no inquisitive follower was in sight. Andrei spoke hastily.

'There's at least one listening device in the flat,' he warned her. 'You remember that fellow who came to fix the electricity last week. I checked after he'd gone. And I very much suspect the telephone's tapped. They won't have heard anything dangerous yet but from now on be careful.

'I've an idea for getting a message to you safely from Finland, so be ready, though I'm not quite sure how yet. That will provide instructions. One more thing. I can't bear not to have a photo of my wife with me in Finland. Several, in fact. Before I leave I'll take some in colour. Have you still got that rather plain dark blue summer dress I disliked so much?' She nodded. 'Get that out and wear it. Together with those reading glasses you've got. They could come in very useful.'

They approached the main door of the building as the clouds spread beyond them, producing an unnatural, almost menacing darkness. They climbed the narrow stairs and he opened the door of their flat.

'It was a bit cold, yes,' he declared in a cheerful voice, 'but I feel much better for it, don't you? Shall we have a cup of tea now and something to eat later or shall we get supper over so that I can get down to that manuscript again?'

ACT 1

1. DOWNHILL SLIDE

Standing in front of the wall-wide double-glazed window of
her mother's first-floor flat, Eeva Arvika was watching the
children playing on the square opposite. Grass-covered in
summer, its Finnish name elevated it to a park and in the
distant spring, still some three months away, seats would
appear on the two diagonal paths and swings and climbing
frames be set up in the near corner. Beyond the square and
a few grid-pattern streets of newish apartment blocks and
the occasional remaining old cream-coloured wooden house,
a paper-pulp factory chimney reared into the cloud-heavy
sky, its banner of dark smoke streaking horizontally south-
ward, carrying to suburbs beyond a bad-egg fragrance which
long acquaintance had made imperceptible to the local
inhabitants.

A bird-pricked covering of hard grey snow had been
crushed down messily on the paths by a confusion of footprints, dog-paw prints and tracks of pram wheels and
'kicking-chair' steel runners to an uneven dark grey mush
of ice. And the winter replacement of swings, the ice-covered
sliding chute, was besieged by chunky thickly-padded in-
fants waiting in an orderly line to hoist themselves up steps,
plummet down at speed and whizz along the ice-track below,
gaining early experience of downhill skiing while themselves
in a horizontal position.

Eeva was fantasizing. Her husband, Peik, had agreed to
having a child, just one would have been enough, and he or
she was one of the happily absorbed toddlers below. Eeva's

mother was taking care of him or her (she would really have preferred a girl) while Eeva was pursuing her singing career across the world. Now she was spending a short break between tours with her mother and daughter (who was the six-year-old in bright blue now sliding down head first). Somehow Peik himself had no part in the fantasy though she could hear his snores and occasional mutterings from the next room. And some of the fantasy was reality: a visit to her mother during an all-too-short break in opera performances and concerts from Berlin to Sydney to Tokyo. Only there had never been a little girl who enjoyed experimenting and never would be. Never had been because Peik had never wanted her and never would he because she had at last decided she couldn't take any more. Better or worse, loyalty, countless resolutions to understand and forgive notwithstanding, she had had enough.

And simultaneously a part of her, remote and critical, looked on sceptically. It had all happened so often before: maudlin self-pity produced by bitterness and above all exhaustion, seeking an outlet. Her marriage after all had been only a small part of a supremely successful career; she was adored by her admirers and extolled by critics and public, while Peik slipped steadily downhill, coarsening in appearance, aggressive, unreliable, unsavoury: a has-been whom managers and selection committees almost invariably passed over.

It was a last-minute, last-hope concert offer, a substitute required for a younger singer incapacitated in a skiing accident—the irony did not escape Eeva though it wouldn't have occurred to Peik—that had brought them a few days before to Oulu, Eeva's earlier home, a utilitarian sensible northern town on the estuary of a sprawling, much-polluted river. Her mother, who since her husband's death had worked in the dispensary of the local hospital, now occupied a three-roomed flat and welcomed her daughter, though hardly her son-in-law, on the few occasions when Eeva had enough time to visit her.

With the door to the next room ajar, she could now hear faint movements. She had been up since six that morning when she had heard the taxi draw up outside, the slamming of its door and then of the main door below, dragging uncertain steps on the stone staircase, fumbling attempts to locate the keyhole so that she finally got up to open the door herself. Bleary-eyed, sour-breathed, without any awareness of her being there, Peik had groped through hall to bathroom where he had retched and vomited over bath and floor and then with sightless deliberation found his way to the bedroom. Having solemnly and carefully removed his fur hat and placed it on a bedside table, adjusting its position to dead centre of the surface, he had collapsed on to the bed and within two minutes was snoring in oblivion. He mumbled in unconscious protest as Eeva removed his boots and by methods learned from frequent experience his over-coat, though he showed signs of waking when she attempted to take his jacket off and she left it at that. Momentarily she speculated on who had dealt with the homecoming Don Giovanni after nights on the tiles: an unfortunate valet or Leporello himself? Kept awake by a guilty conscience, she meditated as she sought the rocking-chair in the sitting-room. Whoever thought up that joke?

Just as well Peik was now beginning to show signs of life. Already past four, and by half past six at the latest he must have survived the torments of coming to, undressing, a shower, a shave and something to eat, and be waiting, resplendent in evening dress, gardenia in the buttonhole, for the taxi which would take both of them to the concert hall in time for the recital billed to start at seven o'clock.

At least he was out of bed now, stumbling about the room, cursing incoherently as he did so. The door was suddenly flung inward, crashing against the side of the bed, and he stood there, his eyes clenched shut, a Samson gripping the two sides of the doorway as if intent on tearing down the pillars of the Philistines in Gaza. His bellow of rage, 'What have you done with my whisky?' ended in a near-whine as he clutched his head in his hands, releasing it again immediately to grab the doorway before he could crumple downwards. Huge, unkempt, unshaven, with bloodshot eyes and the smell of sickness and stale alcohol wafting from him, he glared at Eeva. 'Where've you put it?' he rasped, in a cautiously controlled voice of fury.

'On the top of the medicine cabinet in the bathroom,' she answered coldly.

Afraid to yell or make the least violent movement, he spat out, 'Emptied?'

'There's enough left to put you on your feet. There's also Alka-Seltzer and aspirins, though you should have sense enough not to mix all three. It's now quarter past four and the taxi's ordered for half past six.'

He stood there swaying, hardly aware of what she was telling him. 'Dear Donna Anna—' he intoned her title with loathing—'so moral, so upright, so righteous—' he stumbled over the consonants—'the noble and forgiving wife who cares for her pitiful wreck of a husband.' His voice softened, an actor's blend of sentiment, self-pity and mockery. 'My charming little Zerlina that I adored. Oh yes, there she was: pretty and alluring and ambitious and sly. You know, I really believed I'd found someone different: a soul-mate, a partner, a sweet companion. And I, Pygmalion, created my Galatea: I taught and trained her and made her into the star of La Scala, of Covent Garden, of the Metropolitan. And then I made the absurd mistake of marrying her. And Zerlina transformed herself into that she-monster Donna Anna screaming for retribution.' Carried away by growing nausea and pain and above all by the corroding bitterness of his inadequacy and misery, he was discovering a sustaining relish in creating the part of the wronged and misunderstood husband and artist. 'Yes, my dear love,' he went on, his mind scratching away at the still open wound of his wife's selection and his rejection for the cast of the forthcoming Savonlinna Festival. 'I'll sit there in the courtyard—if I'm allowed even that much share in the performance—and I'll applaud the artist I fashioned, my superb creation, you and your lover Ottavio, that spindle-shanked, mimsy-whimsy pansy of a Finn.' He rolled out luxuriously the esoteric English adjectives he had always delighted in accumulating.

An actress herself, caught up in her own private drama and carried along by a tidal-wave of disgust and fury, Eeva matched histrionics with the full sweep of melodrama. 'At least he's not a spineless, drunken, degenerate has-been that I've been supporting and coddling for years because he's too feeble-minded to look after himself,' she declaimed, torn between Lady Macbeth and Donna Anna and drawing inspiration from both. 'If he'd been my lover, would I have waited night after night for you, undressing you when you're too repulsively drunk to know where you are even, setting you on your feet again when you're incapable of doing it yourself? Would I have put up with your ridiculous affairs and liaisons, any woman of any age or degree of attraction to add to the list, the neurotic adolescent trying to prove himself to be a man? Would I have used my salary to keep a fatuous object like you in comfort who's called on to perform only as a very last resort? And now I tell you, my useless, unsavoury, conceited, contemptible parasite of a husband, as for months and years I've been waiting to tell you, I'm leaving you, leaving you, leaving you, and you can make your own journey to hell.' The savage joy of this emotional release swept her into her mother's empty bed-room where she flung herself on the bed sobbing in uncon-trollable relief.

When at last she calmed down, she went towards the bathroom to wash her face but found the door locked and heard the splashing of the shower inside. He could look after himself, it seemed. Her mother would be home in an hour and would get him something to eat: her only need was to get away, to walk freely in the cold air and work out her next moves. Her absence from the concert would cause comment since as a celebrity she was to sit among the town notabilities, but Peik would doubtless furnish an excuse: one of the few things he was really good at. She dabbed at her eyes with a tissue: their puffiness would be attributed to the outside temperature of $-18°$, and scribbled a note to her mother which she left in the bedroom. 'Sorry. Called away unexpectedly. Back soon.' She slipped on her sable coat with matching hat, stepped into sealskin boots and left the building.

As she turned in the direction of the river, flurries of tiny ice fragments, driven by the north wind, stung her cheeks. She exulted in the sheer cruelty of the wind which shared and challenged her own fury, and with her mind empty of thoughts strode over the sand-blackened ice-coating of the pavements. The children had all now been fetched home in the deepening gloom but it was still light enough for her to enjoy the immense slate-black snow clouds sweeping dramatically towards her from across the river. She was an avenging Valkyrie riding into battle, a Brunnhilde charging across the heavens: it was Wagner, not Mozart, who understood the human soul.

The vast snowfield that was the estuary stretched into distant darkness: she turned right again in the direction of the town, watching her feet more carefully on the uneven slippery riverside path. The cold, which was gradually penetrating even the layer of protective fur, was sapping her mood of triumph: As she struggled to keep upright, she recalled her hazardous slither over Lapland ice ten years before: even then his juvenile exhibitionism had ended in near-disaster for him. On that occasion he had kept his word though, arriving one day after the appointed date at her flat door in London, a huge bouquet of red roses in his hand. How he had wheedled her address out of the music school secretary she never learned. He had invited her out to dinner the same evening and then had more or less taken over her singing tuition for the next two months, eventually dragging her off to Hamburg with him where he was booked to sing Don Giovanni the following autumn and inducing the producer to offer her the part of Zerlina. Other rôles had followed, at first less demanding ones like that of a Papagena, and, as her voice had matured, the prima donna parts: Mimi, Butterfly, Tosca, with himself as Scarpia.

By this time they were married, though now, some eight years later, she hardly remembered how it had come about. Despite his widely-publicized determination to surpass even Leporello's list of Giovanni successes, his early interest in Eeva had been restricted to her singing. It was only after her first notable success as Mimi that he had suddenly declared that he had loved her since the first time they had met, had indeed worked himself to death to secure her fame and fortune and would now, as he put it, claim his reward. He swore he would take their marriage vows completely seriously though perhaps he wouldn't bind himself to the occasional 'temporary distraction' in the far-distant future when she would have equal 'recreational privileges'. Undeceived but infatuated, well aware that she was deluding herself in imagining that unselfish devotion might achieve miracles, she had accepted, and was in no way surprised when no miracles were indeed achieved. She had even had the wild hope of at least cutting down his drinking, but as all his other old habits reasserted themselves, his drinking and unreliability increased, marring his performances and infuriating managers who had to call on understudies and substitutes on the many occasions of the 'indisposition' of their star principal.

Eeva walked along the bank which was indistinguishable at a distance from the river below, past a solitary fisherman still crouched over his hole through the ice and to landward a huddle of old wooden salt-houses brooding in winter abandonment. Beyond on the waterfront a palatial modern theatre and a luxury hotel gazed at each other in self-conscious admiration, and in incomprehension at sky, ice-lidded river and the long bridge carrying people and vehicles from south to north, from forest to the wilderness that would inevitably outlive them.

Chilled by the wind and damp from clinging snow, Eeva moved towards the pool of light. The cold had numbed her passionate fury, leaving her empty and depressed. Defiance and resolution with their intoxicating sense of power and self-sufficiency were easily dissipated, she was realizing, but what should they have been leading to? What was she actually going to do?

As an honoured guest she had recently been shown round the new library by one of its consultant architects, special attention having been devoted to the music department: books, records and audio devices. At the present moment however it was the café that lingered in her memory, some-where she could relax, warm up and enjoy a coffee over a magazine.

Now I really must make plans, she resolved as soon as she had installed herself. But the comforting warmth after the freezing walk and the long-term effects of a sleepless night were inducing a pleasant drowsiness in which nothing specially mattered. She sipped her coffee, forcing herself to concentrate at least on the immediate future.

First I must book a room in the Vaakuna Hotel for tonight, and then as soon as he'll have left I'll go home and talk things over with my mother. I'll leave again about nine: I feel so worn out and he won't be home before morning. Mother can lock her own door in case he starts demanding to know where I am: she could put the main door on the chain even, if she feels like it. I can leave a message at the hotel reception that I'm not to be woken up whatever happens, just in case he guesses where I've gone.

Her mind reverted to her present surroundings. But what is to become of him? She nagged herself. Mother certainly won't let him stay with her and anyhow he wouldn't. He'll have none of the money left that I gave him at the weekend. Somehow her head persisted in leaning back against nothing and she would jerk it to the vertical without even realizing what she was doing. Finally, in a daze she left her table, took another chair and pushed it back against a wall. Letting herself down on to the chair, she immediately fell asleep.

She was awakened by a hand on her shoulder. She looked up into the face of a kindly middle-aged woman, one of the library assistants. 'Oh,' the woman said, 'it's Miss Ruuskanen, isn't it? I mean Mrs Arvika. I'm afraid we're closing now. You were having such a nice sleep.'

Eeva sat up in confusion, looked around the now-empty café and started to apologize profusely, while getting up to find her coat. 'Don't worry, dear,' the assistant consoled her. 'I do hope you weren't intending to go on to the concert. It must have started some time ago now.'

'It doesn't matter,' Eeva stammered in embarrassment. What would the woman think of her? Hardly that she had over-indulged, surely. She scurried towards the stairs, was let out by a side door and set off for home, completely forgetting her booking at the Vaakuna.

One or other of the parallel main streets was the shortest way home and she set off along the nearest. Its pavements were illuminated by shop-window displays, some of which seemed to have changed little since she had lived in the town as a child, though now as on every evening of the week the road itself was blocked by an endless procession of cars. Fathers' cars mostly, purloined by the gilded youth of the city to drive for the next two hours round a narrow rectangle of central streets for some purpose she could never discover, except on rare occasions it seemed to pick up a girl with equally restricted ways of passing the evening. A frontier town on the edge of nowhere, she thought, as she turned a corner towards her mother's flat.

Her mother, a small grey-haired woman with a cheerful birdlike face, was finishing off the washing-up as Eeva burst into the kitchen. She glanced sharply at her daughter before speaking. 'I was wondering where you'd got to. Not at the concert, that's for sure. Why don't you take your coat off? I suppose you've had more trouble from him, haven't you? Prancing home when the rest of the world's getting up. You weren't the only one he woke up.'

'This time I've really made up my mind, Mother. I've had enough. I'm leaving him.'

'Take that coat off,' her mother reminded her. 'You'll ruin it wearing it in the kitchen, however clean I keep it.' She opened the fridge door, raising her voice slightly as Eeva moved into the hall. 'It's turned even colder: minus 22° now and falling. You want something to eat, I suppose. I'll warm up a couple of meat pasties and some bouillon, and heat some water for tea.'

'I really mean it, Mother,' Eeva said, as she returned.

'That doesn't surprise me,' her mother retorted. 'You know what I think without my telling you. There'll be twenty better men who can start hoping now. If you don't go back on it, as you've done so often before. I got him a meal before he went off.'

Perched on a high stool, Eeva was cutting bread: she felt more than usually hungry after her excursion. 'How was he?' she asked almost casually.

'Quiet, unusually quiet, and almost polite. He actually remembered to say thank-you when he finished.' The rigid Finnish convention, which Eeva observed automatically even when abroad and often to her embarrassment.

'Did he need much help?' she asked.

'None at all. He was already shaved and dressed when I got back. And he even called his own taxi, though he did look a bit sickly maybe.'

Eeva put down the knife and went to the bathroom.
'Strange,' she commented, as she returned. 'He hasn't
touched the whisky I left for him. He must have got some
hidden.'

Neither of them spoke until the food was on the table and
Mrs Ruuskanen was handing her daughter a cup of hot
water with a tea-bag in it. 'What happens now?' she asked.

'He can open the door for himself tomorrow morning,'
Eeva said. 'And I know you've got sense enough not to do
it for him. I meant to book a room in the Vaakuna and
forgot but I can telephone when I finish eating. I've made
it quite clear to him I'm going. I'll get the plane to Helsinki
tomorrow. You do understand, don't you, Mother?'

'And what am I supposed to do with him?' Mrs Ruuskanen spoke with resignation rather than reproach.

'I'll leave enough money for him to get through the next
week or so,' Eeva said. 'After that it's his lookout. He
certainly won't want to stay in Finnish Oulu. And he equally
certainly won't be awake in time for the plane I'll be on.'

'And after that?'

'Goodness knows. I ought to file for a divorce but I'm
due in Vienna next week. I'll talk to some lawyer in Helsinki
before I go, but that's not very satisfactory, I know. What
worries me, Mother, is what's going to happen to him. No
money, no job and no one to turn to.'

'Serves him right,' was her mother's comment. 'It's not
your business any more. Remember that. He's long ago lost
any scrap of claim he's got on you. And everybody will agree
with me. So don't worry about that.'

'It's not the publicity that worries me. It's just that he's
so helpless. He's just a child.'

'You're the world's biggest fool, that's what you are. You
can't still be in love with him, that's certain. Maybe it's
been having you there that's stopped him growing up.'

'We'll see, I suppose,' Eeva said wearily. 'Have you got
any cheese I can have with this bread? I'll pour myself

another cup of tea and then I'll phone the hotel. What's the time?'

'Coming up to nine. There's a Haydn concert on the TV starting at nine. You needn't leave before ten at the earliest.'

But it was ten minutes before the concert ended that they heard a key in the door and a few seconds later Peik was standing before them, bringing with him a waft of the crisp night air. His cheeks glowing from the cold, his hat clutched in his hand, he bent to kiss Eeva with tender concern. 'Where were you?' he asked gently, gazing down at her anxiously. 'Everybody was so worried about you when you weren't there. I kept looking for you while I was singing but you still weren't there. You're not ill, my dear, are you?'

He removed a glove and laid his hand on her forehead, slipping an arm round her shoulders. 'No temperature at least,' he said, and withdrawing hand and arm and taking off his coat, he turned off the television and sank down at her feet, looking up at her like a repentant small boy. 'Eeva,' he said caressingly, his voice richly deep with carefully-targeted emotion, 'I'm sorry. I'm sorry. But you do know me by now, that I say things I don't mean when I feel terrible and I was feeling terrible. My head was all hell and not only from the whisky, and I was hating myself too.'

'How did the concert go off?' Eeva asked coldly.

He stood up, exultant. 'It was superb: three, four encores, imagine four encores from Oulu Finns. The audience loved it and so did I. If only you'd been there, *kulta*.' Eeva recoiled suspiciously at the use of the Finnish form of darling, but he failed to notice. 'Listen, I've got a taxi waiting outside. Paavo is expecting us at his house and everyone's dying to meet you. Change now, presto, prestissimo, my girl: I give you ten minutes.'

He took hold of her hands to help her to rise, his eyes clearer than she had seen them for weeks and sparkling with amused admiration. Pulling away her hands, Eeva regarded him thoughtfully. The naughty boy asking mother's forgiveness yet again? No, this time there was something more to it. She spoke decisively:

'And be left to make my own way home some time after midnight or with luck be brought home, if anyone's capable, with everybody sorry for the unfortunate wife whose husband has somehow got lost—at the same time as someone else's wife?'

He withdrew slightly, a shade of cold anger momentarily crossing his face. Such uncalled-for indifference to his brilliant theatrical talent! With chin tilted slightly, he gazed in soulful reproach. 'Anna,' he said, correcting hastily, 'Eeva, that's not fair. All right. It has happened before, occasionally, when I've drunk overmuch perhaps and there's been —temptation. And we did agree, you remember.' He turned to face her squarely. 'But I can promise one thing. I'm keeping off all alcohol from now on and women too, if it's possible,' adding the last words for himself, Eeva thought. 'You know I really looked at myself in the glass this afternoon and saw myself as I am, and as you must always see me. And now I've got a career to remake. And what's much more, there's you to win back, Eeva, *kulta*, darling. Try me, Eeva, just this evening: you can always walk out on me tomorrow if you still feel like it.'

So he had sensed her determination, and had no intention of letting her go. As an indispensable meal-ticket? A mother-figure to cling to? A sacrificial lamb to torment? Eeva found her images getting somewhat confused. Partly because of the irrepressible hope and longing: could he possibly be sincere? Still feel some genuine love for her, faced with her loss? Could there be the smallest possibility of their rebuilding their marriage, or maybe creating it for the first time?

Poor silly Donna Elvira, she reflected silently. However she was treated by her Don Giovanni, however much she persuaded herself she hated him, she was there waiting, clinging to absurd hope. I'm no Donna Anna: she didn't have any childish illusions: I've been billed for the wrong part.

'The taxi, Eeva,' his voice broke in. 'Your blue dress. It goes so well with your adorable blue eyes.'

'Oh, stop hamming,' she said as she got up. 'You're worse than a TV commercial. I suppose I can't let them down. But if I have to leave without you, that's the last you'll ever see of me, outside a theatre or the divorce court.'

With their principal guest accepting only fruit juice and the musical élite of Oulu, deprived of an example by their cosmopolitan betters, hesitating to overdo things, the party never really got off the ground. Realizing that one of the Opera Festival selection committee that had rejected him was present, Peik consented to sing: an aria from *Boris Godunov*, another from *Rigoletto* and finally, with every bit of his former charm and magic and mastery, the Don Giovanni serenade. He flirted distantly with most of the ladies but reserved his full charm for his own wife, who had apologized prettily for her absence from the concert. They left soon after midnight, to the obvious regret of everybody present.

It was a remark he let fall in the homeward-bound taxi that provided some enlightenment to Eeva. 'By the way,' he said casually, 'I picked up something interesting in the interval during tonight's concert. That poor guy they selected as Don Giovanni at Savonlinna was run in by the police last week for driving under the influence. Poor devil. He'll get six months at least. Of course, there'll be the understudy they've selected, but with half the committee out of the country for the next month or so, they won't get round to deciding who'll understudy the understudy, will they? Not for the time being, anyhow. I wasn't too happy about tonight's performance you know. I think I'd better put in some practice. And of course we'll be together at Savonlinna when rehearsals start, won't we? And—don't laugh—I've decided to take up jogging.'

Could this overweight prematurely-aging figure beside

her, with his sagging chin and dark-ringed puffy eyes, still have the illusion of renewed fame and admiration, of actually being considered for the Festival, Eeva wondered. Was this the reason for his touching revival of interest in his wife: he could hardly present himself at Savonlinna as the estranged husband of the leading prima donna. As so often before, she realized his mind was quietly following hers, but as he chuckled contentedly and his arm went round her, she hardly cared.

Oh, foolish, fond Elvira, she almost said aloud, how well I understand you! What a pity I've got the wrong kind of voice to do proper justice to your part!

2. COFFEE-TABLE TALK

On the wide verandah which ran the length of the Turunens' country home Iris lay relaxed in a garden chair, gazing across the tranquil lake towards the old ridge road. A little to the right where garden met water stood a traditional red-painted wooden sauna and from somewhere in front of it could be heard boisterous splashings, plunges and yells.

Ritva Turunen, oculist wife of a specialist in internal medicine, appeared with a large coffee-pot which she put down alongside the fragile Arabian coffee cups, the rice china cream jug and sugar basin, the tea plates simulating cracked ice and the sweet bread pulla, biscuits and gooey glazed fruit sponge.

'Enough sauna for one week. Time they joined the ladies,' she declared, and herself yelled lakewards, '*Kahvi on valmis,*' interpreting automatically and needlessly for Iris, who had heard it scores of times before, 'Coffee is ready. We'll give them five minutes.'

There was an answering yell, the sound of bodies thrusting

their way through water and then of feet slapping up wooden stairs on to the sauna verandah.

Ritva let herself down into a chair with a sigh of relief. She looked tired. Her consulting room formed part of her large flat in Savonlinna, two rooms of which were used also by her husband for his private practice which he carried out in addition to his consultancy duties in the hospital. During the week they often had to stay overnight in town with their two school-age children, but they spent as much time here as they could, even though this meant extra housework. 'There isn't a quieter place even in Finland,' they would say, 'birds and the lapping of water, with maybe leaves rustling in summer—that's when our windows are open— and nothing at all but the log fire crackling when they aren't in winter.'

'It's a pity Markku and I had to miss our lesson last week,' she said to Iris. 'We wanted to hear what you thought of Lahti.'

'I'd been there before, you know,' Iris responded. 'Still very much the city of today, Finnish design, though it's probably grown a bit since I last saw it. This time Ilmari merely met me at the station, took me somewhere for a meal and whisked me off on a twenty-four kilometre walk.'

'That's an extraordinary way to behave.' Ritva would happily ski forty kilometres in the depths of winter but it would never have occurred to her to tramp even four kilometres in summer except to gather mushrooms and berries. 'Did it have something to do with his nature preservation campaign?'

'Yes, it did. There were some eight of us and we were trying out a forest, field and lakeside path project for a Nature Trail Scheme Ilmari wants to inaugurate.'

'How very Germanic!' Ritva shuddered slightly. 'I think of heavy boots and lederhosen and backpacks. But it's very like Ilmari, with his love of wild life and Finnish nature. Do you meet often?'

'We've seen each other only about four times, including today when he collected me in Savonlinna. We're both too busy.'

'Is that what he says? He's a wise person, Ilmari, and subtle. We've known him quite a long time. I think he understands you rather well. You don't want to be rushed, do you? And he knows it.'

Iris was pondering an appropriate request for an explanation which she was not sure she wanted when four figures with lank wet hair, bright pink faces and wearing slacks and sweaters emerged from the sauna door facing the house and tramped in single file towards the verandah.

In formal dress and on suitable occasions, the first of them would appear an impressive figure: tall, lean, a finely-moulded intelligent face with keen blue eyes and silver-grey hair. Today Dr Markku Turunen had reverted to his youth. Stamping on to the verandah, he raised an arm and greeted Iris with a 'Hei, Iris! Sorry the four of us were already boiling ourselves when you two arrived. You've certainly seen friend Ilmari before but not surely the other two. Please meet the world-famous genius among opera directors who has dropped in from somewhere beyond—' he waved vaguely across the lake in an easterly direction—'to inspire us here in this tiny Finnish town. He is Dr Andrei Pavlov and this, Andrei, is our friend and teacher Miss Iris Lawton. She's also Ilmari's friend: probably the reason he was late today.'

Somewhat to her surprise, the burly genius representative of the egalitarian Russian proletariat bowed low over her hand and then kissed it, making her feel an unworthy Queen Victoria. The other stranger was presented far less formally as Risto Aho, 'our Don Ottavio'. Exceptionally shy for a theatre performer, he flushed even pinker, shook her hand while avoiding her eyes, and muttered something inaudible which might have been his name. Ilmari merely reminded her,

'Iris, you now see the Finn at his moment of greatest glory. For an hour he's done nothing but boil himself—not far below a hundred degrees today, Centigrade naturally—and almost simultaneously frozen himself in water that was until two weeks ago solid ice. And having cleansed body, mind and spirit empty of every idea and scrap of intelligence, he knows he's king of the universe. That coffee smells good.'

'Then you'd better get some inside you.' Ritva was already pouring it into the cups. 'Alcohol for talk: coffee for ideas. Or have you forgotten why we invited you? Not just for your company. And speaking of company, how are you getting on with this year's guardian angel, Andrei?'

'Worse than the devil himself, who might at least be entertaining. They wouldn't admit him even to hell: he'd bore the very flames to extinction. A block of petrified wood with pivoted limbs made for the goose-step and a mouth that can open only downwards, for eating, talking and snoring. Even in the next room his snores keep me awake at night, while his non-stop talk sends me to sleep in the day. He lectures me interminably on the magnificent achievements of our mighty Soviet Fatherland, not forgetting his own indispensable contribution to their success. He then proceeds to demolish the West, including Finland, quoting facts, figures, statistics, opinions, most of which I know to be absurd.'

Ritva offered the cream which he waved away impatiently. 'And where is he now?' she asked.

'I'd like to think he's still asleep, though he's probably already got the local police out in search of me. I insisted on taking him for a long walk this morning, for the good of my overstrained nerves on the first free day we've had from rehearsals. We were late back for lunch which was large and heavy, starting with ample vodka and finishing with ample brandy though not for me, and then retired to our rooms for a nice rest. I'd already arranged with Eeva Arvika to invent an excuse for phoning me at three-thirty: that gave him twenty minutes to drop off. She rang at exactly the right time to say she'd lost her copy of the score and could I possibly let her have another one immediately as she wanted to practise. Naturally I left quietly so as not to disturb any of the hotel guests. He'll turn the town inside out when he wakes and scream at me when I get back but Eeva will confirm my story, including the fact that Peik delayed me by inviting me to sauna.'

'Can Peik be trusted?' It was Markku who asked.

'All he knows is that I needed a bit of relaxation. He'd certainly confirm my story if it helped to persuade the committee to consider him the official understudy. I don't think there's much doubt they will: he's pulled himself together remarkably: polite, considerate, actually ready to listen to other people. He attends every practice, agrees with every suggestion I make. And it's a thousand to one it's all for nothing.'

Risto set down his fragile cup with a violence that startled their hostess. 'He's hardly considerate to his wife,' he almost shouted. 'He's spiteful, jealous, and gives her hell. Only a saint would put up with it. She can't still be in love with him: she just says she sticks to her promises. She should have left him years ago. He only married her to make a prima donna out of her and add to his own reputation. And now she's at the top and he isn't, he doesn't like it. One of these days when he bullies her I'll—'

He broke off, bringing his clenched fist down on the table, jarring the crockery. Ritva shuddered and whispered, 'Please, Risto, my cups!' The others regarded him in silent sympathy. Everyone knew that this shy and awkward thirty-four-year-old with a magnificent tenor voice but inhibited acting ability had idolized Eeva for years. Markku spoke gently. 'He really isn't very well you know. Don't you think we'd better get back to the subject you came to discuss?' Looking even more embarrassed than usual, Risto relapsed into obscurity.

Andrei nodded. 'You understand I must leave rather soon. And this is almost certainly the only time when we can decide things together. When last year we discussed the possibility of my staying and my wife's joining me, I said I'd think about it. Now, as I've explained to you, something's got to be done, and I myself can't see any way of doing it.'

Ritva tried to imagine herself in Natasha's position. 'You're quite sure your wife will be willing to go through with it?'

'Certainly not willing. For her the West is spoilt, immoral, the empire of Babylon. I suggested to her that she might be able to do something to reform it. More to the point, I convinced her that it wouldn't be a welcome committee that would greet my return. We don't get on so badly, you know, maybe because we don't see much of one another. Anyhow she agreed that life in Russia without me would be worse than life in the West with me. She'll keep her word. You mentioned the possibility of crossing the border on foot when we discussed this last year. Do you still consider that feasible?'

There was an awkward silence while everyone gazed towards the lake now rippled with gold from the invisible orange of a sun low in the sky on the other side of the house. Andrei waited patiently, rightly doubtful whether amid the demands and distractions of doctors' and singers' lives anything more than the minimum of consideration had been given to the optimistic ideas and suggestions of the previous year.

'Well now,' said Markku, neatly tossing the ball elsewhere, 'Risto comes from Parikkala, rather near the frontier, and must have done a fair amount of hunting and skiing in that area. The general picture isn't very hopeful, I know, but would you say there would be any possibilities in that field?'

Charged with giving an opinion, Risto lost his shyness.

'There may be a very few people who make it their business to know something about that area,' he said, 'though if there are any, I know nothing about them. The locals keep well away from those parts: there've been too many cases of hikers, usually strangers to the area, who've wandered too far and haven't returned until after a considerable time and a good deal of fuss. It's obvious there's no Berlin Wall there or fortified fence as in Central Europe. It would serve little purpose: even if you can make it into Finland, you've still got a hell of a long way to the Swedish frontier and genuine protection.'

'Would you really be handed back if you were discovered before?' Iris wanted to know.

'I don't know. The authorities would deny it. They'd refer to obligations under the Geneva Convention and to the Russians who already have been granted asylum. But a lot of ordinary Finns have other ideas: Finland's "special relationship" with its neighbour and the like. Asylum is said to be far more readily granted in Sweden and it's usual to make for there.'

Andrei nodded thoughtfully while Markku resumed his speculations.

'No Berlin Wall, as you say, but I suppose other what would be called "protective" devices on the Eastern side of us: mines, dogs, guards, wire, searchlights and the like.'

'There could be, plus a few more they've thought up,' Risto assured them. 'Nobody really knows and unfortunately they haven't thought to publish maps indicating their exact positions. And the no-man's-land area can be twenty kilometres or more wide, with just three official road crossing-points.'

'Rather what I thought,' Andrei summed up. 'Hopeless so far as Natasha's concerned.'

'Isn't a small boat possible?' Ritva asked. 'Surely in clear weather you can actually see some of the Russian islands from the coast at Kotka.'

'And how would you get from the Russian coast to the islands?' her husband asked impatiently. 'You can be certain the whole area is thick with observation points, guards, gunboats and every other offensive and defensive device imaginable.'

'Leaving us with three official road crossing-points with no possible way of getting through them,' Andrei summed up despondently.

'Why not?' Ilmari, the only one who had been giving the matter serious consideration for some weeks, had been waiting for this opening.

Dr Turunen eyed him with satisfaction. 'I'd been hoping for something from you,' he commented, and turning to Andrei explained, 'Ilmari is of Russian parentage. Not much help in itself, but he's bilingual and has always been curious about his father's homeland. So as a Finnish-born subject, before he started playing around with animals, he used to act sometimes as courier to Finnish coach groups visiting Leningrad.'

'I still do occasionally when I get a bit fed up with my own country. It seems such a paradise to come back to.'

'And that's why we've invited him today. Apart of course from the pleasure of his company and acting as chauffeur on this occasion for Iris. He told us on the phone he had an idea, so go ahead, Ilmari.'

'Why not substitution? That's why I asked you to bring photos, Andrei.'

'You mean Natasha takes the place of some Finn returning in a coach?' Andrei had in fact already considered this himself but decided it would be impossible. 'How about all the identity checks? As thorough as any in the world.'

'Not always quite so thorough as you might think. Basically we have to get the cooperation of a woman of about your wife's age: within five or six years, shall we say. The same with regard to height and build, though she'll be sitting in the coach for the two main passport checks. Hair colour, style and length similar to those on the visa photo. Lightly-tinted glasses possibly to conceal any variation in eye colour.'

'The other passengers would notice the difference,' Ritva put in.

'She'd have been the unsociable type. Wouldn't have mixed much with the others in Leningrad. The woman next to her would be in the know, though as far as the others were concerned, they'd have met only on the journey. As for passport checks, there are usually two: one shortly after leaving Vilpuri, the other some twenty-two kilometres later, just before Finland. One guard goes to each passenger sitting in the coach and examines the passport while the other stands by the door, I suppose to grab the unmasked fugitive as he tries to run for it. There's a Customs check too when everyone leaves the coach and goes into a building to have his luggage very thoroughly checked. Meanwhile some of the boys are inspecting every separate centimetre of the coach itself. There are metal detectors too and currency declarations but they don't seem so interested in passports at this stage. Actually it's the Finns who seem more careful: they carry off the passports of foreigners to their office, I suppose to check for undesirable aliens. If the person in question hasn't shown undue agitation by the time the passport is returned, he's let through. Or maybe if he doesn't look too relieved at having made it. If you're on the Lappeenranta road, there's a café a kilometre or so inside the frontier where the group enjoy Finnish coffee again but nobody would be much surprised if one passenger was feeling a bit poorly and her new acquaintance stayed with her to cheer her up. Come to think of it, later when the whole thing comes out, that may set a problem as the Finnish police will want to question the new acquaintance: we'll have to try and find a Finn who normally lives in Sweden. That shouldn't be too difficult, I think.'

All eyes were on Andrei whose bristling eyebrows were

puckered ominously. After a moment of suspense, he responded unexpectedly mildly, 'There is indeed a small possibility that it will succeed. There is just one insignificant matter you seem not to have considered.' His voice hardened as he stared coldly at Ilmari. 'The consequences for the unfortunate lady left behind.'

Ilmari had indeed considered these at some length and, though far from satisfied with his conclusions, was aware that he would have to give an impression of optimism. 'From her photos, your wife appears to be a homely sensible middle-aged housewife,' he said, 'hardly likely to be taken for a glamorous secret agent. Any substitute who resembles her will obviously be the kind of tourist who walks into trouble the first day of her visit to another country, getting her handbag snatched, mislaying her passport or traveller's cheques. Stupid but undoubtedly respectable. And she'll be well prepared with her story.'

Andrei scraped back his chair, his head tilted back, his arms flung wide in a gesture of utter incomprehension. 'And you who are supposed to know something of your father's country,' he roared. 'Do you think the KGB will pat the stupid housewife on the head, tell her she's been a silly little girl and send her back in the next bus?'

Ilmari regarded Andrei reproachfully. 'She'll be there two weeks, months, years perhaps. She'll be interrogated, jailed, interrogated again, get what's usually known as the full treatment, especially in a case like this. However good her story and however well she can act the part. The Finnish consul is likely to be actively discouraged by his hosts from interfering: nor will a lot of helpful information be made available to representatives of the Finnish Press.'

With his hands now on his knees and his head bent forward, a sarcastic smile on his face, Andrei commented, 'I'm sure you will have a long queue of middle-aged housewives who resemble my wife and look completely stupid, at the same time having a greater acting ability than Garbo and more powers of invention than Mark Twain and who are craving for KGB interrogations and jail sentences for an indefinite period.'

'She could make a fortune from the tabloid press in other countries,' Ilmari could not refrain from commenting. 'No, there isn't much of a queue yet. But,' he added with more hope than certainty, 'you undervalue the toughness of our Finnish women. Also their courage, humanity and imagination. Have you the photos of your wife with you now, Andrei?'

With slow deliberation Andrei drew the three from his wallet and handed them to Ilmari. Natasha faced him squarely, her dark hair cropped short, heavy-rimmed glasses concealing most of the upper part of her face, determined mouth and jawline. The two showing head and shoulders could have served as passport photographs, and like these, catching their subject at her worst, were little more than distortion of the reality, which could have been applied to any of at least a quarter of the women of her age. Ilmari passed them round to the others.

'Within a week we must somehow or other have located and persuaded someone who could be taken for this woman, can be trusted and is far from being as stupid as she looks. If you accept this possibility, Andrei, that is to say. Or can you suggest a better one?'

The silence that followed was eventually broken by Andrei. 'You're chasing shadows. You'll find nobody. And if a miracle happens, how do we brief Natasha?'

'No need to worry about that. I can easily do that myself as a group courier. With my small part at the beginning and end of *Don Giovanni* you won't need me for rehearsals till late in June, will you? I'll make a special request to the tourist bureau, tell them you need some music from home urgently.'

'You realize that any obvious contact with Natasha will be noted? My home is bugged, you know.'

'Well, well. They must find you interesting. I've got a vague idea already: some kind of memento from you that they won't question at the ingoing Customs. Strange things they seem to dislike there: Bibles, for example: they must be quite terrified of a nationwide religious revival. A woman I know had the cross-stitch embroidery she'd got with her to do on the bus scrutinized for a couple of minutes: maybe they mistook her for Madame Defarge. But I doubt if they'll question . . .'

He was interrupted by the telephone, over-dramatic it seemed in the present state of tense conspiracy. Ritva picked up the receiver. Her replies were short and alarmed and she gave worried glances at Andrei.

Replacing the receiver, she spoke hurriedly. 'That was Eeva. Your companion has missed you and has been telephoning to everyone who might know where you are. When her turn came Eeva told him you'd brought her some music she'd asked for and was now in the sauna with Peik. He'd be bringing you back to your hotel in about half an hour— she didn't want to give him time to come to the house and check. Ilmari, could you take Andrei back to Savonlinna at once?'

'Of course. I'll drop him at the car park where Peik would leave his car if he were going for a meal or a drink: it's near the hotel but his arrival with me won't be noticed then. How much we have to deceive, alas! I'll have to go straight on to Lahti from there as I'm due back by ten. Iris is spending the weekend with you, I understand.'

'We'll be taking her back tomorrow night,' Ritva assured him. 'But if the road's busy this evening, it could take you half an hour to get to the hotel, so you really must get going at once.'

Andrei sighed. 'Back to teacher,' he said, as he rose from his chair. 'I fear the naughty boy is due for a scolding. We can discuss things further in the car and you'll be coming to our first full rehearsal on Monday, won't you, Ilmari?'

'All being well, certainly. Allowing for free time between twelve and two. And you too, Iris, my love. No lessons, appointments, arrangements, not with the President himself: I'm booking a table for Monday lunch at the Casino Hotel. Till then I take my leave, taking a useful lesson from Andrei.' He took her hand and kissed it rather more lingeringly than Queen Victoria might have approved, shaking his head as he released it. 'Just what have you been thinking about for the past ten minutes?' he continued. 'Not me, I'm afraid. If only it had been.'

The two men having been hustled out, Iris began clearing away the used coffee-cups, her mind obviously on other matters.

3. MIDSUMMER FIRES

Few nations on earth would celebrate Midwinter Eve, though this would seem a time for optimism since the sun's retreat has again been halted. Yet in the northern countries of Europe it is Midsummer Eve that is the time of rejoicing, even though it signals the departure of the sun for the other side of the globe and henceforth every day must lose minutes of precious light.

No one in Finland who has a summer cottage, or at the very least friends or relatives with one to stay in, will wish to remain in town on Midsummer Eve, unless of course he prefers the silence of empty town streets to the noise of an overpopulated countryside. A few solitary, shambling figures who have already enjoyed their private celebration of the festival lurch in their own pathetic universes from side to side of the pavement and elderly ladies on their way to have coffee with stranded friends of their own age steer clear of them easily enough after a lifetime's practice. Smoke associated with factory chimneys now issues only from wood fires, cars have mysteriously disappeared and the Finnish nation has reverted for one night in the year to its distant country-dwelling past.

Kaarina Laufach, blonde, buxom and in her early forties, had been born in Joensuu, to the north-east of Savonlinna and was indeed a typical Savolainen, practical, plain-spoken, kind-hearted and realistic. Her solid, equally capable and sensible husband was German, an architect from Frankfurt, who had designed and arranged for the construction of a large, rather pretentious villa near Koli on the shore of Lake Pielinen and not far from Kaarina's early home. It was now their habit to spend at least part of the summer there and return for skiing in early spring. With a highly-trained rich mezzo voice, Kaarina had secured a contract in the Opera House in Frankfurt and had seemed a natural choice for the part of Elvira in the Savonlinna performance of *Don Giovanni*.

Shortly after the start of rehearsals, Kaarina had invited the various members of the cast to a Midsummer celebration at her villa and had included the Turunens and Iris, who, now that her teaching for the session was over, had taken on a job as guide to English-speaking visitors to the Castle. Andrei had been notified that his presence was requested at the Midsummer reception given by his ambassador in a villa near Helsinki and that a car would call at his Savonlinna hotel to provide transport for him and his companion-guide. He had duly departed in the early afternoon. Most of the others had promised to turn up at Koli and the Turunens were bringing their two young sons.

Ilmari was to pick up Iris at her home in Savonlinna, but leaving Lahti in mid-afternoon, he found he was a unit in a crawling file of cars, most of them driven with unaccustomed caution by harassed fathers, supervised by mothers and crammed with excited children and possibly elderly relatives besides. When he eventually arrived half an hour late, it was to find Iris propping herself against the wall of her apartment block, studying the already-encountered Finnish Grammar, though he had the impression that rather few pages had been turned since he had last seen it.

'Hallo,' she said. 'Happy Midsummer, if that's what I ought to say. I thought it was you I saw coming some time ago and I came down in anticipation. It hardly seemed worth going up again and it's such a nice day, isn't it? And then I remembered I'd left the Grammar in this case: it's the one I had in Lapland. Why must you use a singular form of the noun after a number: like saying there are one hundred and twenty minute in two hour?'

'You say in English "It cost ten pound", don't you?' said Ilmari, picking up the case and putting it into the car boot. He had left the passenger door open and Iris slipped in. He got in himself and started the car. 'Sorry, I was late,' he said. 'You're not still stuck on cases of the noun, are you?'

'I've heard fierce arguments between Finns about certain partitive plural forms,' Iris informed him, 'so surely I'm justified in taking my time getting things quite right. Have you had a busy morning?'

'Not at all. Not even a colic. Probably the fine weather, though there's thunder on the way. But I heard something interesting this morning. I'll tell you about it when this traffic thins out a bit.'

They drove along peacefully with occasional comments on surroundings, impressions and speculations, though, keenly sensitive to Iris's most carefully-concealed moods, Ilmari was aware that she was slightly ill at ease and nervous, apparently of himself. At close on eight o'clock the air was still warm—the afternoon temperature had touched thirty —and the atmosphere was uncomfortably sticky and humid. In meadows that broke the monotony of forest and lake, the hay was awaiting stooking while roadsides and uncut meadows were thickly speckled with multi-coloured summer flowers.

Ilmari's decision to postpone his telling of the 'something interesting' was reinforced by what could be described as 'environmental conditions'. With the town behind them, the windscreen was soon being spattered with the tiny bodies and wings of myriad insect swarms, summoned into the open by the coolness of evening and the reddening sun. As countless as particles of blown sand or storm-driven raindrops, they coated the windscreen, the transparency of their massed wings shattering the already dazzling light ahead. Whenever the unscreened road curved towards the north and west, Ilmari was blinded by a furnace-red sun with its light fragmented by the thick iridescent film coating areas inaccessible to wipers and hazing over the glass being cleared.

'I'm glad we don't have to walk very far this evening,' Iris commented, 'we'd have been gobbled up.'

But already there was a slight shiver among the leaves and in the few places where trees allowed, they could glimpse cloud beginning to build up on the south-western horizon. It was not long before the shiver had strengthened to a breeze which swept up and carried away most of the insects, allowing them both to relax and think about other things.

Even so the silence that had fallen between them continued, Iris gazing out at the unnatural lifeless daylight which had usurped the evening darkness completely, Ilmari infected by his companion's uneasiness which for once he was unable to interpret. Finally after they had left Joensuu behind, it was Iris who spoke.

'You know, I feel we don't belong here,' she almost whispered. 'We've been enveloped by another universe, an alien galaxy in which we're intruders. Everything feels different, uncanny, as if all life and personality has been drained out of it. I once saw a film in which all forms of life had been destroyed by a high-pitched sound, but everything else remained untouched: I suppose today it would be a neutron bomb. And everywhere stood quite empty and unchanged, utterly beautiful and utterly impersonal—like this.'

'The white night of the Northern countryside,' Ilmari responded. 'You've only experienced it in the town, I suppose, and there are always human sounds there. I often walk in the forests at night—well protected against insects, I must say. There's so much to see: plants and trees rising out of ground mist, the bright pinpoint lights of glow worms —I think that's what they're called in English. And it's far from silent there. Above all, of course, there's the singing of the night birds and the squeaks and rustling movement of animals and smaller creatures. Occasionally I've chanced across a lynx, glaring down at me from a branch. It may all resemble another universe but you're just seeing this world differently: the night world seen in daylight; that's why it's so unnatural.'

'I prefer an alien universe: it all feels alien. Do you ever take a camera with you?'

'Yes, I do. And I carry medicines to relieve sick and injured animals. Some are in such pain that I'm forced to put them out of their misery. But mostly I enjoy watching, especially animal families with their young ones playing, though it takes a lot of patience waiting until they've forgotten they've heard you coming.'

He paused, staring ahead at the restless leaves and the rippling deep blue water of the lake they were passing.

'Iris,' he said quietly after a few minutes, 'what are you planning to do next autumn?'

He had an odd feeling that she was relieved at the content of his question, had in fact been afraid of being faced with something else that she would have had difficulty in countering. She answered without hesitation, 'I hope I can come back to Savonlinna, for a year anyhow. I've been very happy there.'

'How about Lahti?' he asked, treading it seemed with considerable care. 'A week or so ago I happened to mention to the director of a large pulp factory that I knew a very capable English teacher living in Savonlinna who might possibly welcome the chance of teaching in a city that's larger and nearer Helsinki.' Iris was already surveying him with upraised brow but he continued serenely and undismayed. 'He's got a large estate house not far from my village and we've got acquainted through the ailments and injections of his pedigree collies.'

'Really!' Iris interposed acidly. 'And is it for himself or for the collies, Scottish I assume, that an English teacher might be needed?'

'Rapped on the knuckles for interfering in things not my concern. I'm unrepentant. When I ran into him this morning, he informed me he'd been discussing the matter with staff members in his company and there'd certainly be work for someone, teaching at various levels and also helping with English correspondence and the like. There'd be a small furnished flat available in the buildings used for staff accommodation and you'd be entitled to low-price meals in the canteen. Hours would be short and he'd recommend you to plenty of other pupils if you wanted. Pay would be reasonably good, I'd guess.'

There was a considerable pause with Iris's brows now creased in a frown before she responded,

'It's a bit sudden, you know.'

'That answers a proposal of marriage, not the offer of a job. You'll have to wait for the proposal until I've more hope of its being accepted.'

'And I suppose this job is the spider's web to enmesh the unwary helpless fly?'

'Of course it is. I can't hypnotize you all the way from Lahti to Savonlinna: or is a snake even less alluring to you than a spider? Would you prefer the psychological approach: you are to be conditioned into enthusiastic acceptance.'

'Maybe that's what I'm really afraid of.'

'It wouldn't be so bad as all that,' Ilmari protested mildly.

'No beatings, no kneeling on the floor to receive the hat of your lord and master. I'm not even all that fussy about the honouring and obeying, though I would like a little affection at least if you can't manage love. I'd be willing to share the household jobs, and I'd take your independence for granted: free time and holidays to spend as you wish, though it would be nice if you'd include me sometimes.'

'You make it all sound so wildly romantic. Could you lend me a pen to write down all conditions and concessions for you to sign? On second thoughts a bit premature, perhaps: the proposal I understand is to follow the conditioning. But just a few minor matters for you to browse over during the coming months of separation. Couldn't it be perhaps that we're both a bit too elderly, too independent, confirmed in our undisturbed contented ways? I've more than a suspicion you'd soon find me an irritant, jangling your sensitive nerves, while I might be afflicted with immortal longings for Kathmandu or Outer Mongolia or islands far away.'

'And if I took up singing full-time again and we travelled together?' Ilmari was concentrating on the road ahead.

'You know that's no good. You'd be longing for your cows and collies and I'd be hating myself for dragging you away from them. Oh dear! Why didn't one of us decide against a Christmas in Lapland?'

'We'd still have met in Savonlinna. At the Turunens. You can't escape your destiny, Iris.'

'Destiny is what lies ahead of one so obviously nobody can escape it. But you're making it sound like a trap I can't avoid walking into. Free and uncommitted, I have the illusion that I can shape it just a bit. Midsummer fantasy maybe. Give me a few cold rainy days to think it over, will you?'

'Of course. By the way I'm leaving early Monday morning with a tourist group going to Petroskoi. The Turunens say they've found a suitable woman and she understands the job and its unpleasant possibilities. I'm a bit worried as they now seem to be underrating them. But we haven't got much choice and she's ready to take it on. So Andrei and I have been preparing the instructions that I'll pass on to Natasha.'

'Not, I presume, in the company of the indispensable comrade?'

'Oh, we've been in the small control office behind the stage busy with staging and technical problems, recording and the like, and there we've been left alone while he hovers in a strategic position on the battlements and sits in the theatre. We get to Leningrad the same day, take the night train to Petroskoi, spend two nights there, back to Leningrad overnight and arrive in Savonlinna on Friday evening. After that, intensive rehearsals. We can discuss the job again then, and also if you like when we're at the Edinburgh Festival in August, though maybe that's leaving it a bit late.'

'You'll need at least my telephone number in England. What can I find to write it on?'

'Don't worry now. We'll have plenty of time before you leave.'

'I might forget.' There was a sense of urgency about Iris's search for pen and paper. She could find only the Finnish Grammar and the pencil she had been marking it with. 'I'll use this,' she said, 'I won't be needing it in the near future. There, it's on the cover. You can give it back when we next meet.' She scribbled the number and slipped the book into the open glove compartment.

Ilmari glanced sharply at her before staring stonily ahead without answering. Iris was just nerving herself to make a confession that would inevitably bring fire and thunderbolts on her defenceless head when he swung the car into a small parking area overlooking the lake, leaned across to open her door, got out himself and fetched out the cases. He strode towards a narrow path which descended steeply towards the lake. 'We'd better hurry,' he said noncommittally. 'It's after nine and they won't light the bonfire till we're there. The path's not easy but it's the shortest cut.'

They had to scramble down the rough uneven path, which was dry and slithery from the drought, suddenly swerved, twisted and dropped round exposed tree-roots, and was sown with small pebbles which trickled downwards under their feet instead of supporting them. Clutching the two bags, Ilmari strode down regardless of hazards: he seemed to have forgotten Iris's existence. Iris slid, edged sideways and grabbed at brambles, reaching the lakeside garden, a tree-ringed forest clearing, to be greeted by familiar friends and introduced to new acquaintances. It was Ritva Turunen who did the honours, Ilmari having disappeared with her husband immediately on arrival and Kaarina being busy in the kitchen.

They had indeed been expected for the past hour and Kalevi and Timo, the Turunen boys, who had been charged with the honour of setting light to the great fire, were fidgeting impatiently. The fire had been built on a small rock isthmus, the obvious creation of an artist skilled in the fretwork architecture of the Midsummer bonfire, with logs great and small, branches, brushwood and kindling positioned to produce an inflammable mountain. On each shore of the lake, bonfires were already ablaze, their smoke borne eastwards and northwards before the rapidly freshening wind, which had already driven massive purple thunder-clouds almost to the zenith.

The kindling of the Midsummer flame attracted a fair number of spectators from kitchen, rowing-boat, verandah and water's edge, though several were missing. Peik was said to have departed half an hour before on his daily jogging routine, and Risto was believed to have joined Markku and Ilmari nobody quite knew where, though all of them had been seen five minutes before in the sitting-room in earnest conversation. So it was Raimo Metsälä, whose straw-blonde hair and round fresh face fitted him ideally for his part as

Masetto, who kindled the torch to hand over to the boys while Ritva, Eeva, Syvi Keskinen (a rather earnest-looking Zerlina), and Iris, were the attendant priestesses. Somewhat buffeted by the wind and casting uneasy glances at the advancing clouds now devouring the sun itself, they had the duty of acclaiming the first eager flame. Within a few seconds it had multiplied ten and soon a hundredfold while the boys cheered and danced, almost falling into the lake in their efforts to view the farther side.

As she turned away from the flames, Iris caught sight of Ilmari as he emerged from the back of the house and, with a face as stormy as the clouds above him, climbed swiftly and surely the path she had almost tumbled down. Unnoticed, she broke away from the group and followed, her earlier uncertainties almost forgotten in her anxiety to catch him. When she reached the car park, she found him standing at the parapet fence looking out over the water, his hands clenched at his sides. A line of cars on each side of the space and parallel with the parapet faced inward to where a long wooden table with benches attached had been installed for picnickers. Between the cars nearest the path and the parapet, a few tree-stumps, shaped and smoothed to form additional seats, were arranged in groups of three or four. Iris promptly collapsed on one of them not far from where Ilmari was standing.

'Obviously getting old,' she gasped, breathing slightly more heavily than she needed to. 'There was a time when I could have skipped up that path like a mountain goat. And now what's the matter with you?'

He came across and stood glaring down at her. 'You know,' he snapped uninformatively.

'Look,' said Iris, 'why don't you sit down? That would put us on an equal footing, or should I say sitting? That stump you're standing in front of is slightly lower than this one and we can glare much more effectively at each other at eye level.'

She ignored him as he lowered himself reluctantly, while she gazed through the vertical bars of the parapet at the restless pools of orange flame reflected in miles of deep blue water far below. Long low forested islands, pointed at their ends, drifted in lines of three or four to the invisible ends of the lake, so that most of the fires on the far shore could be seen only as reflections against the sky. After a long silence during which she was aware that the wind had momentarily subsided and the lull before the storm had calmed even Ilmari's fury somewhat, she said serenely, 'This is the evening I've waited for most of my life, actually from the first time I'd ever heard of the existence of Finland. A teacher at school—I suppose I must have been about eleven at the time—had been on holiday there and she described to us the Midsummer bonfires reflected in each of the thousands of lakes. That was when I fell in love with Finland and knew I had to go there.'

Ilmari who had been looking down at his feet, almost as if trying to repress an unwilling smile, raised his head again to gaze at her face as her eyes travelled over the lake and then caught sight of the distant lightning flashes flickering above the horizon on the far side of them. 'And now, perhaps you'd tell me what I'm claimed to know,' she requested.

He jumped to his feet impatiently, only to resume his seat at a gesture of her head. 'You can't do it,' he said authoritatively. 'It's out of the question. I forbid it.'

'To honour and obey, and we're not even married yet, if we ever were to be. All right. I won't quibble. I didn't mention it before as I didn't want to spoil the ride—you might have been told already anyhow—and when I did try, it was too late. You're sore first and foremost because it wasn't you I discussed it with before anyone else. One reason for that was that you just weren't there, so how could I? And the second you're making quite clear now: it would have been a waste of time trying.

'Let me tell you what you'd have said if you'd had the

chance,' she went on. Her tone changed to that of a pedantic headmistress "In undertaking the role of substitute, you're putting yourself into a situation you're utterly unqualified to deal with. You don't speak even one word of Russian. You've never set foot inside the country. You haven't the faintest idea of the callousness, the tenacity, the cold-blooded ruthlessness—a lot more—of the KGB and police officialdom. You're a nice respectable middle-aged English lady of blameless morals and sheltered life, in which the police exist to tell you the way, see old ladies across the road, find lost dogs, and in extreme cases investigate bur-glaries. They address you even in the most unlikely event of their having to arrest you as madam and allow you to summon your lawyer to protect you during any questioning. For all you know there may be a list of prisoners' rights and privileges hanging on every cell door. You're neither very bright, beautiful, resourceful, crafty or hard-boiled: on the contrary, you're the prototype of the innocent abroad".'

'In addition, you're downright stupid, pig-headed and ridiculous, though I'm not so sure about the innocence.' The wrathful Commendatore himself towered above his unrepentant victim with the flames of Hell around him. 'Are you so dissatisfied with your life that you want to spend the next twenty years of it in a Russian jail? Somewhere near Outer Mongolia, I suppose, or one of the off-shore Arctic islands far away. And do you—'

'No, I don't, however that question might have ended. I'm scared rigid, if you want to know. I've thought of just a few of the risks all right. Do you want me to run away because I'm scared, with nobody in the least likely to take my place? Incidentally, I didn't notice all this concern when you were proposing a Finnish sacrificial lamb: it was you who suggested her, wasn't it?'

For a moment Ilmari stared at her blankly, a look of horror on his face. Then he sank back on to the unwelcoming tree-stump, muttering, 'How right you are! It didn't seem

real then. I was carried away by an idea and the risk didn't
seem important in comparison with freeing Natasha.'

'Who from all accounts isn't much interested in the idea.'

'We'll have to cancel the whole thing,' Ilmari continued,
hardly listening to her. 'It isn't so very important after all.'

'Only likely to cause separation, grief, suffering for years
whether Andrei returns or stays. And what might be
Natasha's position if her husband decides to remain in the
West?' Iris had moved a few yards away and was now
standing with her back to the parapet. The huge cloudbanks
had overwhelmed the last traces of daylight: lightning
streaked across them incessantly while thunder muttered
and rolled, warning of the imminent assault. The wind had
momentarily dropped and forest, lake and field huddled in
silent foreboding.

Caught up in the surrounding drama and having some
difficulty in resisting a touch of melodrama herself, Iris
pressed on with the attack. 'If we're still here in not much
more than five minutes' time, we'll have to swim down to
the house. So I'll waste no more time arguing.

'If anyone on this earth can manage to survive the wrath
that must descend, I'm the one. Just because I am what I am
in stark literal truth: middle-aged, dumb, homely, gullible,
English—all utterly genuine and all the interrogations and
truth drugs in the world wouldn't reveal that I was anyone
else. I'm handmade for the part of the gormless English
woman tourist—no one else anywhere can equal her sim-
plicity—who gets her handbag snatched after one hour in
Paris, Naples or Rome. And her passport pinched in Viipuri
in ten minutes. That would never happen to a Finn, would
it?'

'And because you're a half-witted Anglo-Saxon they'll
believe every word you say and send you straight home?'

'After an interval and some arm-twisting, it's not absolutely impossible. I'll be terrified at first and tell all I know
that's fit for their ears but by the third time through I'll

stand on my rights and refuse to open my mouth until they bring me the British consul, who'll turn up reasonably promptly, always provided it isn't Sunday and he's spending the day at the seaside. I've got a mother, two sisters and a brother who'll besiege the Foreign Office and the local MP when I don't return on the due date: I'll have let them know about the Russian venture before I start out. Have you any friends in the BBC, on a national paper or even in the upper levels of the British Council who could start some agitation —I'd leave it to you how much you tell them?'

'I suppose those of us in the know may be able to collect a few. You'd want a few sensational headlines and news items, I suppose. Something on the lines of "Pavlov Defection: British Woman Tourist Held by KGB".' Ilmari was again being carried away by an idea, his opposition apparently forgotten.

'Something like that, with the spotlight on age, respectability and helplessness—though I wish my own name didn't have to appear. I'll hate the publicity. She'll have been mugged or drugged—nobody's quite sure—and her passport stolen. And when she's rescued or complains, the police arrest and imprison her. Not very encouraging to the British tourist contemplating a quiet holiday in the Soviet Union. Much more important, there's the trade delegation visiting Moscow shortly and the Prime Minister's projected visit for a general softening-up session. Questions at least would be bandied about in high quarters. Rather more concern, I feel, than a Finn in such position might raise.'

'But you'll have come from the most sensitive point, Savonlinna, from the very side of the central protagonist, Dr Andrei Pavlov himself. They'll never swallow that extraordinary coincidence.'

'There's a very slight risk that somebody somewhere will remember having issued me with a working permit several months ago and report it to the Finnish police. Nobody in the town will know who's involved because everybody knows

me as Iris, which is only my second name. I keep quiet
about my unfortunate first name which would be the one to
appear in any press reports. Otherwise so far as Finnish
police inquiries will be able to ascertain, I'll have arrived
in Finland only a week or so before from England.'

'You couldn't have.'

'Why not, if I've returned to England between—I've got
time enough to do that? My mother's pretty tough and I
think I can tell her the whole story: I'll need her help in
cooking up a story about how I've been spending the past
year—just in case the British police should ask. A small
private school in London, perhaps—there are plenty of
them. I'll leave after a few days, with my British passport
issued in London three years ago, and travel by train to
Travemünde in Germany and thence by boat direct to
Finland: they can inspect my passport on arrival and there'll
be a record of my boat passage, if they need it. I'll travel
around by train, visiting different places and then in Mikkeli
I can go into a travel office to ask for general information
and see one of those brochures about bus trips to Russia. I
can ask for a translation and decide to book on a trip a week
or so ahead. I can get a visa in about ten days and they can
take a photocopy of the important bits of my passport for
it: I've asked about that in a Savonlinna Travel Office. And
for the visa photos I'll make myself look as much as possible
like those photos we saw of Natasha.'

'And Natasha herself?'

'Markku will tell you anything you don't know tomorrow.
I think you've got most of what matters already. You or
Markku will collect her at the coach stop in Mikkeli, parking
a bit down the road, so that you're not noticed. She'll arrive
only a day or so before the last performance and she'll be
staying in that spare room that forms part of the Turunens'
sauna building.'

Iris was shouting now against the thunder and a tempestu-
ous wind which was adding to the drama of noise and light.

Large raindrops were already spattering down on them and were multiplying into a downpour, almost into a vertical flood. They turned to find shelter and as Ilmari glanced back at Iris just behind him, a lightning flash lit up a line of cars. A vivid picture of the nearest car remained on his retina as they raced for the path and a corner of his mind was working away at it as they clung to one another trying to keep upright on the slippery descent through the rain, tempest and near-darkness.

When they reached the garden, he gave Iris a push towards the house, saying, 'Go in and get dry. I've just realized something,' and turned back to climb the now almost unnegotiable slope.

Seeing no reason to argue, Iris let herself into the kitchen where she was met by a horrified Kaarina and taken away to change into dry clothes. Five minutes later Peik turned up, looking in his black jogging outfit not unlike a seal emerging from a pool. He said he had just come out of the forest on to the wider and longer track descending to the house when the heavens had opened. Leaving a pool of water on the sitting-room carpet, he also disappeared to change.

Ilmari was in even worse condition when he arrived, covered in mud and limping slightly from having slipped on the downward slope. He apologized, saying he'd remembered he'd left his car window open. Later he cornered Iris for a moment while she was helping to clear away the dishes and said in a low voice, 'Do you remember that red Mercedes near where we were talking?'

'Yes, there was one, I think,' she replied, 'but I didn't much notice it.'

'Neither did I at the time,' he said. 'It was that flash of lightning that showed it up. It had a Helsinki number plate and I'm almost certain it was Peik's. It had one of the side windows open. I've a thing about leaving my own car windows open and I'd have noticed it, I think, if it had been

open when I first sat down facing it. And when I got back
there to check again, it was closed.'

'So Peik could have been inside while we were there and
left just after we did.'

'He's not such a dedicated jogger as he makes out. I
suspect he'd slipped in for a nap, curled up on the back seat
and opened the window when he heard us talking, just out
of curiosity.'

'So he could have heard what we were talking about.'

'Some of it at least, especially the last bit when we had
to shout.'

'But surely he can't do much about it, even if he really
was there.' Iris was trying to reassure herself. 'Andrei could
be useful to a reformed Peik if he stayed in the West—he
speaks quite highly of him nowadays and Peik knows it. I
don't think he'd be specially interested in anything of this
kind and he's not so spiteful as to give away information for
its own sake.'

Iris was called away to the kitchen at this moment and
dismissed the matter from her mind. At least Ilmari was
partially resigned to her undertaking, probably because he
realized there was nothing he could do about it except to go
back on his promise to carry the instructions to Natasha.
But later in the night when she was kept awake in the small
room she was sharing with Syvi by the noise of the rain, she
realized for the first time the full implications of what she
had let herself in for. Even if she were sent back from Russia
to her own country, it would be years before she would feel
at ease again in Finland. How could she, when she had
made it clear that she had had no previous connections with
the country or anyone in it? An application for a working
permit would certainly awaken memories. Her departure in
a few days' time would mark the end to so many friendships.
Even if she and Ilmari did actually meet in Edinburgh, the
job in Lahti would hardly materialize now.

Before drifting into sleep, she thought she heard a telephone ringing. Next morning three of their party were missing. A tree struck by lightning had fallen across the roof of Ilmari's house. During the night, he, Raimo and Markku had set out by car to see what could be done in time to ensure Ilmari's departure for Petroskoi on Monday morning. It was still raining and the tattered remains of the great bonfire had been washed into the lake. Only a soaking black burned ring remained. Everybody in the house seemed low-spirited, and Iris above all felt that the midsummer of her contentment had passed and she had little but darkening days of isolation and danger to look forward to.

4. COMMUNICATION FROM BEYOND

Summer had come early to Petroskoi: in late June heat the leaves were already losing their spring freshness and the sky its cool deep blue. Natasha was stowing away her morning's shopping: fish fresh from the lake, some of the new crop of potatoes, carrots and peas, rye bread, cheese, lettuce: now her husband was away she had much less to carry. Just as she was finishing, the telephone bell rang.

'May I speak to Mrs Natasha Pavlov?' The Russian was perfect but the deep voice was unfamiliar.

'I am Mrs Pavlov.'

'Good morning. I'm Ilmari Karhu from Finland acting as courier to a group of tourists visiting Petroskoi from Savonlinna.'

'From Savonlinna?' she exclaimed a little breathlessly. 'Where my husband is directing an opera?'

'I was introduced to your husband just a few days ago and when he learned that I'd be visiting Petroskoi this week, he was overjoyed. He'd been making a special tape for you at rehearsals, the principal arias for the most part, but you can also hear him directing and advising. He thought it might amuse you. Posts from Finland can be a bit slow so he asked me if I could deliver the cassette to you personally. He has also included commercial tapes from Britain of the whole opera, which are said to be the best of their kind.'

'What a wonderful idea. How very kind of you to bring them! Would you be able to come here for some tea? I've also got some very good brandy which I'm sure my husband would recommend.'

'I'm sorry but today I have to spend the whole time with the group and tomorrow we're taking the hovercraft across the lake to Kizhi Island.'

'Oh, that's one of the most fascinating places in Karelia,' Natasha broke in. 'It's really the old and very beautiful Russia, with the reconstructed wooden houses . . . But you'll have a lot to do. Can I come and collect the tapes at your hotel. Is it the Karelia you're in? Any time of day would do. I'm on holiday now.'

'Why not after lunch?' Ilmari suggested. 'Service is a bit slow but we should have finished by a quarter past two and the bus doesn't leave till half past.'

'That will be ideal. But how can we identify ourselves?'

'There may be several buses outside the hotel but I'll be standing in front of the one nearest the building. Your husband showed me a photo he's got of you and I look like what I am, a Russian Finn, so we shouldn't have any problems. Oh, and he wanted some notes on *Don Carlos* he said he'd left in a desk drawer.'

They were both some ten minutes before time, Ilmari being the first. He glanced at her with recognition as she approached and they shook hands, moving slightly to the far side of the bus apparently without being aware of it. Out of earshot, Ilmari spoke quickly in a low voice.

'We haven't much time. Andrei told me your phone was tapped and there are always one or two watchers somewhere around this hotel.' He broke off as a woman came round to their side of the bus, almost certainly Finnish from her appearance but causing Ilmari to continue smoothly in his normal voice, 'Yes, he says everything is going splendidly though there are the usual rehearsal problems of course. Ah yes, the notes. Thank you. And I've got the cassettes somewhere here. I'm sure you'll enjoy them.'

He fished in his pocket, bringing out a large, obviously commercially-produced box securely wrapped in its original Cellophane and a single boxed cassette of the type used for home recordings. It was labelled *Don Giovanni Extracts: Savonlinna*. He handed both of them to her and as the woman had now gone on her way, said quietly, 'They took the homemade one away at the frontier and returned it some twenty minutes later. You could see from the position of the tape they'd obviously been trying it out. What you must listen to is Side B of the first cassette of the commercial recording. The first ten minutes will be quite normal: then the message starts. We overlaid the original of course, and then wrapped it quite professionally. Do you understand?'

She nodded and he continued cheerfully, 'Look, I'd like to offer you a coffee. There's a small bar in the hotel.'

Avoiding any solitary bystander, chattering groups presenting no particular danger, he went on quietly with his advice as they walked. 'Andrei says you have an earphone attachment for your set so as not to disturb the neighbours, so listen to the important tape with that. He suggests that the bathroom is the room most likely to have no bugs— though even there you can't be sure. If you listen in there with the earphone attachment, there shouldn't be much danger. You can play the Savonlinna tape and the other parts of the commercial one as loudly as you like: that's side A of the first one and both sides of the other. It would probably seem more natural to listen to the one he's made specially for you as soon as you get back.'

He was leading her towards the hotel steps as he spoke, saying as he passed the nondescript man who seemed to hover around there much of the time, 'Yes, your husband was telling me how much you both enjoyed Kizhi: what a pity you won't have time to join us there tomorrow.'

An attractive man, she thought as they sipped the coffee, charming and yet remote as if his thoughts were elsewhere and they were unhappy ones. Shortly before half past two he put her into a taxi which took her to her flat.

Back in her own home, reaction set in. She took the two boxes out of her handbag, the one labelled in ink and with no covering, the other, the deadly one it seemed to her, gleaming and apparently untouched in its shining Cellophane wrapping, a time-bomb that even now might be ticking to destroy her. The very walls, with their hidden ears, seemed now to have developed eyes as she tore away the transparent covering and peeled away the sticky paper that still sealed the square box. On the cover a benevolent-looking Duke with Italianate-trimmed beard was lifting his liqueur glass. Her thoughts went back to the meeting with Ilmari: surely it had been very dangerous to hand things over in the open like that. That woman, for instance, might have reported what she had seen to the police. They might be at her door at any minute to search the flat. They'd find the so-called 'presents' from the man they suspected already, take them away, examine them thoroughly. And she, the recipient, would face immediate arrest and imprisonment. She must find somewhere to hide the box: in the cellar storeroom, under the bath, inside the fridge? As if they would miss such obvious places! And how much worse it would be for her if she implicated herself further by trying to hide anything!

She sank down in a chair by the side of the desk on which a photograph of Andrei was standing. It had been taken while he was skiing: he was coming downhill towards the camera at full speed, his head thrown back and a smile of pure enjoyment and confidence on his face. And at once she felt ashamed. She was getting worked up, panicking even, for nothing at all. If her telephone conversation had been overheard, the police would already know of the existence of the cassettes and would have no reason to doubt their genuineness: she was making a complete fool of herself.

At that moment the telephone rang. She leapt up, moved quickly towards it and stopped with her hand above the receiver. This must indeed be the police, ringing to order her to report at headquarters bringing with her the items she had been seen receiving outside the hotel. No one usually rang her in mid-afternoon. The telephone continued its monotonous summons. They'd know she was at home and would want to know why she hadn't answered: that in itself would arouse suspicion. She lifted the receiver slowly, cautiously, as if it were the head of a cobra, and put it to her ear, unable to speak.

A familiar cheerful woman's voice said with some bewilderment, 'Natasha, is that you?' Olga Dimitrovna, one of her fellow-teachers at the Conservatoire. Sudden relief made her gabble.

'Oh, it's you, Olga. How nice to hear your voice! I'm sorry, I was just having a bit of a rest. I felt so tired for some reason. How are you? And how are you spending your holiday?' She sensed Olga's surprise: Natasha was not one normally to chatter. But that didn't matter. At least Olga wasn't the police.

'I still find a lot to do,' Olga, the practical and capable, replied. 'I just rang to ask you round tomorrow afternoon to a little tea-party I'm giving for a few of the teachers. It happens to be my birthday.'

'Yes, I'd love to come. Thank you so much for the invitation.' An idea crossed Natasha's mind. 'Would you be free now, by any chance? I've just been given a cassette of a rehearsal that Andrei's directing. One of the Finnish coach guides brought it from Finland. It's said to be amusing in parts. Would you be able to come round and listen to it with me, and have a glass of tea of course?'

Olga accepted delightedly, as Natasha had expected,

knowing she was one of Andrei's warmest admirers. Within half an hour, the two women were sitting side by side on the hard sofa, glasses of sweetened lemon tea on a small table in front of them. They were listening to Mozart beautifully sung, with the Pavlov voice interspersing the arias and occasionally breaking into them, admonishing, reproachfully, encouraging cheerfully, occasionally congratulating and more often roaring like an offended lion.

By the time Olga left, soon after five, Natasha had regained all her confidence. That would fool them, the hidden listeners, the lurking intruders, she thought. She was even ready to try out side A of the first of the commercial cassettes. Far less entertaining though it was than what they had been listening to, she had to admit that the quality of reproduction was infinitely superior; loyally, though, she considered the singing in her husband's production was of a higher standard. While she was preparing her supper, she was humming and even singing some of the arias.

Her mind seemed to be functioning more effectively now at least. A half-hour television news broadcast started at nine so five minutes before, she started side B. At one minute to nine she looked at her watch (an unnecessary but enjoyable piece of visual acting) and exclaimed aloud in obvious exasperation, 'Bother, the News,' turning off the cassette and turning on the television. With the earphone attachment ready in her hand, she then quietly shut herself in the bathroom, perching on the side of the bath, and turned the cassette on again at the point where she had just turned it off.

After continuing for several minutes, the music stopped just at the end of the quartet between Giovanni, Ottavio, Anna and Elvira. There was a minute's pause and then her husband was speaking to her, and momentarily she had the sensation that he was standing there at her side.

'Dear Natasha,' the voice was more subdued than his normal one but quite audible—'I'm sure you're sitting not very comfortably maybe but listening carefully and not disturbing our good neighbours—or anyone else. I have a picture of you as I speak, sitting bolt upright on the edge of the bath. And only you can hear what I'm saying.

'When we meet again, it will be in far more comfortable surroundings. My earlier fears have been confirmed. I was summoned to our Embassy in Helsinki a fortnight ago and told that I would be needed in the near future in Leningrad for a production there and would have to return immediately at the end of the Savonlinna season: the Swedish arrangement has been cancelled on that account. There will be no production in Leningrad—that is certain—so I know exactly how things are. I've made a show of pleading to be allowed to go to Sweden and then allowed myself to be convinced of the advantages of working in Leningrad. They think I'm fooled.

'I've already explained the situation to some of my good loyal Finnish friends here and they don't offer to help— they insist on doing so. As soon as possible after the last performance one of them will take me in his car to the land frontier with Sweden. We shall travel by night while my Embassy companion is asleep and should be inside Sweden before he discovers I've gone. Fortunately there's no passport examination within Scandinavia.

'You'll probably be coming by another route: possibly by sea via Naantali, so I shan't see you till we're both in Sweden and ready to apply for asylum together. Now please start to listen carefully. Better not take notes: one never knows.

'The guide who gave you the cassettes has a reliable contact in Leningrad. Next Saturday you'll get a telegram from a friend of your brother's in Leningrad to say that your brother has had a heart attack and may not be able to survive it: he is begging to see you. You can show the telegram if you need any official travel permit and you'll travel by train overnight. Wear the same dress as you had on for the photograph I took and see that your hair is about the same length and style. Take as little luggage as possible.

'You'll be met at the station in Leningrad by a middle-aged dark-haired man, who'll have been shown your photo already and will shake hands with you and call you by your name. Try to look worried about your brother: ask suitable questions about him. I doubt if you'll be checked on arrival or followed, not with your good reputation, but who knows? You'll be taken to a nearby hospital and inside, but you'll leave by another door, get into a parked car and be driven to Viipuri. Your escort will have a suitable story in the unlikely event of your being stopped on the way.

'In Viipuri you'll have to wait alone for a time inside the station but at 2.15 go outside and look out for the arrival of a Finnish coach with Kuopio on the front. It usually comes in soon after 2.30 but one of the passengers will have persuaded the driver to be there a bit early so that she can buy something in the hard currency shop opposite the station. The coach will be carrying Finns who'll have been spending a short time in Leningrad and it stops usually for about twenty minutes (this time I hope for half an hour) to allow the passengers to change their last roubles at the exchange office in the station.

'One of the passengers who will get out by the front door will be about your age, similar build and hairstyle, but will be wearing a fawn coat. She'll be carrying a blue handbag. She'll look up and down and then wander slowly across the street, as if sight-seeing and start to move along one of the narrower streets that branch off.

'Keep close behind her and at a point where there isn't anyone particularly near, overtake her. As you go ahead, pull a handkerchief out of your pocket, together with your keys which will fall to the ground. She'll pick them up and hand them to you. Thank her first in Russian and then in English—she will be English—so that she can understand. Chat for a moment: she'll then ask you for directions and you'll offer to show her the way. Your escort from Leningrad will be hovering not far off, so you'll know which way to turn. He'll be moving off by then and you can follow him casually some distance behind. He'll disappear into one of the courtyards of the apartment blocks round there, where he'll have parked his car, and a few moments later you'll go that way yourself. There'll be a bit of a scuffle apparently when the Englishwoman is forced into the car and you'll get in beside her. The car will move out immediately, and drop you not far from the coach parked outside the station. Meanwhile the Englishwoman will have given you her coat, her handbag with her passport and visa inside it, and glasses which will be very slightly tinted to hide the colour of your eyes. Keep your own glasses in your pocket for later.

'You will make your way to the coach and get in. A middle-aged Finnish woman will stand up, say something to you in English and let you pass in front of her to sit beside the window. There'll be an English book lying on the seat. From now on you're English with no more knowledge of Finnish than you've already got, which I must say isn't much for a Karelian. Without attracting any attention, look through the passport and the visa so that you're familiar with the information there of exact age, place of birth, where it was issued, stamps of countries visited and the like. I doubt if you'll be asked but you never know.

'Read the book and pay little attention to the people around you: the Englishwoman will have kept very much to herself throughout the trip. You could look a bit tired and ill perhaps. The woman next to you, who will be working with us, might address you occasionally in English but you won't have to answer more than a word or two.

'Your passport will be examined twice on the Russian side of the border, once soon after leaving Viipuri and once shortly before the Finnish frontier. Between these checks there will be a Customs examination. There's some twenty-five kilometres from Viipuri to the frontier. When the police get in, one will come round to inspect passports and visas while the other remains at the front. Show little interest when you hand over the documents: you'll be deep in your book and just look up casually at the policeman. If there are several buses returning, there could be a long wait before the Customs office, up to three hours on occasion. Stay where you are and read your book or go to sleep. You'll have to get out to go through the Customs office, taking everything with you, while the bus is searched extremely thoroughly. When you get out you'll collect a blue suitcase from the luggage compartment under the coach: the lady sitting next to you will help you with it, so keep close to her to find out which it is. Use English if you have to speak in Customs: though not many of the officials understand it, I think. The case will contain clothes, shoes, sponge-bag and not much else: the keys will be in the handbag. You'll have to open the case and the handbag too and both will be searched but they won't find anything. You'll also have to present the currency document in the handbag so see you haven't got any roubles anywhere. The Englishwoman will already have got rid of any she had in Leningrad.

'The Finnish frontier post is just inside the border and they'll almost certainly take the passport away from you as it's a foreign one. They probably check it against some list but don't worry about that. Just don't look too relieved when they return it and remember you speak only English in case of any inquiry.

'The coach will probably stop at a coffee-bar a short way inside Finland, but your neighbour will mention to the others that you're feeling very tired and have got a headache, so you won't get out. She may come back before the others with tea in a plastic beaker and a sandwich, and stay beside you to protect you from anxious inquiries. She's a friend of the Turunens who works in Sweden and she'll be returning there by the first possible boat, so if there are any later police inquiries, I don't think they'll involve her.

'You'll still be feeling a bit poorly at Mikkeli where you'll be leaving the coach so she'll help you out, fetch your case and see you down the road a short way where there'll be a car waiting for you. That will bring you to a safe place where you can spend the next two or three days.

'And now back to the music. We meet again in Sweden where I hope those in authority are a little more human than the ones we've left behind. Till then, au revoir my dear.'

The music was resumed while Natasha sat listening but unhearing. Finally she switched off the recorder and returned to the sitting-room. Her earlier terror was returning. This was all too much; she couldn't face it. There would be appalling risks. But would they be worse than just waiting here? Tomorrow she must listen again to the instructions and think out more clearly all the implications. She turned off the television and reached for the cassette: *Don Giovanni Extracts—Savonlinna* and slipped it into the recorder. Just forget for now.

5. TO HIS JUST DESERTS

So far the summer had been superb, with the sixty thousand Finnish lakes (giving or taking a few) serenely reflecting blue skies in unruffled surfaces and with temperatures reaching for the low thirties. In the country retreats rimming the shores of a considerable proportion of the sixty thousand, families dug their gardens, tended their apple trees, gathered wild raspberries—later would come the bilberries and mushrooms—swam, rowed, shattered the peace with motor-boats, sunbathed and even got down actually to reading the handsome leather-bound volumes that in winter might merely enhance the appearance of the sitting-rooms of town flats.

For two weeks in mid-July Savonlinna was crammed with

visitors who were being equally busy in an idle way. They strolled along the lakeside, licked ice-creams, lingered in the open-air market and the temporary souvenir shops or dutifully inspected the various art exhibitions, the Finnish products exhibition, the Finnish countryside photographic exhibition. Each evening, shirt-sleeved or summer-frocked, they sauntered in their hundreds across the two wooden bridges linking the three islands and through the castle gate. After turning left and right a few times they eventually took their places in the truly Great Courtyard. Before them was the immense stage with the two massive flights of stone steps sweeping upwards to doors on high—devilishly slippery, steep and uneven treads which had to be negotiated non-chalantly with upraised heads by bands of priests, courtiers, villagers, citizens, seamen, pilgrims, all in full voice. There was the contented hum of Finnish voices like the murmuring of honey-filled bees in high summer and overall the serenity and relaxation of the Hay Month, as Finns have identified their July.

The evening of the last performance of *Don Giovanni* was no exception, at least in the impressive daylit auditorium. Behind the scenes, however, anxiety, agitation, near-panic prevailed. By 7.40 performers should have been emerging from their dressing-rooms in their full glory, costumed and made-up and with time in hand for last-minute instructions or an exchange of comment, complaints or banter. But the nightmare of every director and every cast had materialized: one performer, and that the principal, was missing. The substitute for the original Don Giovanni, now languishing unromantically in jail, had been a certain Hannu Hietanen, a worthy, technically proficient singer with a good voice and presence: lacking perhaps some of the charm and vitality of the ideal Giovanni but essentially reliable. Inevitably, therefore, it could only have been disaster that had detained him, the suggested nature of the disaster ranging from a fatal road accident, a heart attack, drowning while swimming, to a minor breakdown on his way to the theatre. As this day before the final evening performance had been a free one, no one had seen him since the previous evening and a frantic telephone call to the country cottage rented for him remained unanswered.

Peik was fidgeting behind scenes, moving restlessly between the café, his wife's dressing-room and backstage in general, hovering not too far out of range of the director. He looked white and drawn and somehow hunched together and he stared vacantly at the people milling around as if unaware of what the commotion was about. At one point Eeva, in the rich blue robes of Donna Anna, took his arm and turned him to look at her so that she could examine his face: he could be suffering from one of his increasingly frequent headaches or, she suspected, be drinking heavily again. He shook himself free of her impatiently and looked almost beseechingly at the hurriedly-approaching Andrei, who gave him the sharp order: 'Get into your costume and get made up as soon as you can. Allowing for the overture you've got around twenty minutes. I'll have an announcement made before the start.'

An instantaneous shock of excitement transformed Peik. For a moment he stood rigid, a radiant smile electrifying his face: he then snapped his fingers, yelled at the top of his voice 'Caramba!' and charged for the principal dresing-room, refusing all offers of assistance. The costume he had had made for himself in preparation for some such emergency was stored there, and after only a quarter of an hour he re-emerged in traditional doublet and hose, dark green flecked with gold, and in full make-up. His hair had been kept trimmed and his hair darkened throughout rehearsals and with his old mocking insolence and fascination, he appeared to have abandoned his own personality in favour of the character he was to portray. He bowed patronizingly to Andrei and approached Eeva as she waited for their joint entrance, smiling at her triumphantly before chucking her under the chin and giving her a long exultant kiss. He had been drinking, yes, she thought, but this alone would not account for the wildness and the pinpoint pupils of his eyes or have induced this feverish excitement.

Word had been passed to the conductor to delay his entry while a hastily-prepared loudspeaker announcement was made in Finnish, Swedish, English, German, French and Russian, equally curt and uncompromising in each, and all equivalent to the English version: 'The part of Don Giovanni will be sung this evening by Peik Arvika.'

The prompt arrival of the conductor, who bowed to the somewhat muted applause of a bewildered audience, gave little opportunity for speculation before the first premonitory, threatening and at the same time slightly mocking notes of the overture suggested what was to come.

Leporello, cheerful, middle-aged, competent, with all the appropriate flexibility of tone, but lacking, as any Finn would, the natural South-European guile and eel-like adaptability to depravity in high places, set the operatic ball rolling. He was soon joined by the distraught Donna Anna exchanging vituperations with her would-be betrayer, who forthwith proceeded to make matters infinitely worse by murdering the lady's father, the vengeful Commendatore.

And so the plot uncoiled, Don Giovanni's villainy ever more starkly exposed, and simultaneously the sheer unhoped-for mastery of Peik Arvika's performance more brilliantly manifest. Slightly overplayed indeed: there was an intensity and excitement in acting and singing apparent to the singers, though in this vast open space protected from the sky only by a rainproof canopy, almost certainly unmarked by the audience. This was fiction endowed with life, the archetypal irresistible libertine and egoist, audacious, superbly virile, challenging virtue, justice, humanity, and already irrevocably doomed.

Andrei had hoped to spend at least part of this last performance in the auditorium with the Turunens and their children, but in the present circumstances this would be impossible: he could only wait in his small backstage office for the dreaded telephone call, by now unlikely to come from Hannu Hietanen himself: much more likely from a distracted relative, a hospital or the police. It was rather more than half an hour later that the door flew open violently and, breathless and at first incoherent, the missing Giovanni burst in, supporting himself for a few moments by leaning on the table while trying to give inadequate voice to an explanation.

Andrei helped him to a chair and sent for Ilmari, now off stage until his final fateful re-entry. Still gasping slightly, Hannu asked and immediately found his own answer: 'You've started, then. Yes, I suppose you had to. What's the time?' He glanced at his own watch which had stopped. 'Doesn't matter. I hoped I might make it after all. A neighbour brought me, after he'd patched me up.'

'Patched you up?' Andrei's voice expressed concern. 'You had an accident, then?'

'You can call it that, if an accident can be carefully and diabolically planned.' The door opened quietly and Ilmari came in, looking distinctly odd in an adaptation of a sixteenth-century Venetian senator's robe. He glanced at Hannu, who smiled feebly, and promptly rummaged in a cupboard for a glass and brandy bottle, pouring out an ample portion and handing it over. Hannu gulped down a half of it before continuing: 'He found me an hour or so ago.'

'You were found?' Andrei caught Ilmari's eye in bewilderment.

'By some miracle. I was trussed up in one of those log-built huts they use as stores, just off a field-track not far from where I'm quartered. I was lying on the earth floor, tied up and helpless.'

'But what had happened? How had you got there?' It was Andrei who was continuing the questioning.

'You haven't seen the place I live in, have you? It's a bit off the road; you park your car at the beginning of a thirty-metre track and then walk to the house. It suits me: I can sing as loudly as I like and I enjoy being alone there. Last night I didn't get back till after midnight and as I was putting my key in the door, somebody jumped on me and knocked me out. He must have chloroformed me too, I reckon, because I don't remember a thing more and had a head as heavy as lead when I came to this morning. Whoever it was, and I'm now pretty certain about that, he must have dragged me back along the track—I still bear the marks— and dumped me in his own car, then driven along the road as far as the field track and along there to the hut. I'd noticed it before: it was empty and the door was always secured by a peg pushed through a metal hasp. I suppose he dragged me inside and then tied me up, very efficiently, I must say. I came to some five hours ago unable to move or to speak: I'd been gagged too and had a splitting head- ache. The gag was a rough piece of towelling knotted behind at the base of my skull. What he hadn't noticed—it had been fairly light outside but darkish in—was the head of a nail protruding from a log just above the ground, near where I was lying. I managed to wriggle along to it and get the nail inside the knot, pulling on it gradually until it loosened. I was working on it for some two hours and even now I don't know how I managed it. Then I tried shouting every so often without much hope as nobody much uses the path and at last I actually heard someone coming and I bellowed. It was the farmer who owns the land, my neighbour, and he heard me yelling through the gaps between the logs. I told him what had happened and about tonight's performance as he was untying me and massaging my legs so I could stand. Then he helped me along to his house, prepared a bath for me, patched up some of the cuts and scratches and brought me here in his car. No time to eat anything. He telephoned here, by the way, but got no answer.'

'What time?'

'It must have been about eight o'clock.'

'Just as we were starting, I suppose. But who on earth could have done it?'

'That's obvious, surely. You know as well as I do.'

'But you haven't any proof.'

'No police court evidence. But last night just before I got to the place where I usually park, I'd spotted the back of a car that had been left a short way along a track into the forest. I didn't notice the number, only the colour and make. And we both know who owns a red Mercedes, don't we? Well, he's had his chance as he'd planned, but only till the interval. Then I take over.'

It was at that moment that the door opened and Peik stormed in. He lurched slightly as he charged towards Andrei sitting facing him across the table and the wild unsteady excitement was even more apparent than earlier. Sitting slightly behind the door, Hannu was out of his range of vision, his whole attention being concentrated on Andrei. He hammered his two clenched fists on the table and roared, 'That fool Ottavio is upstaging me the whole time and his singing's atrocious. What the hell does he think he's doing?'

Before he could say more, Hannu moved behind the table and stood there as cold and silent as the Stone Statue itself. Peik stared across at him as though at Hamlet's father's ghost. If only Iris had been here, Ilmari was thinking, how she would have appreciated this real-life encounter between masters of the art of melodrama.

Whatever his physical condition, Peik had by no means lost his ability to take some appropriate emergency action, in this case to shift his target from director and presumptuous fellow singer to the unwelcome arrival.

'Where have you been?' he shouted. 'Do you think you're so important that the whole performance can be held up to such time as you find it convenient to appear? Everything waits for the maestro, does it? And now you're finding we can do perfectly well without you. You're not needed here. Why don't you clear out?' His voice was growing more strident and frenzied as he screamed at the rigid figure facing him. 'You worm your way into a part you're not fit for and then, like the cretin that you are, you lose your nerve. Then you turn up to save your face when it's too late, when you know you won't have to do the impossible. I knew what would happen and I was prepared—'

He was screaming now, without control, his limbs jerking convulsively, a grimace distorting his face, but he was cut off in mid-sentence as Andrei leapt up from his chair and roared,

'Silence! Do you want to be heard by half the audience out there? What have you got to rant about? You've got everything you wanted: by what means the police will inquire later. How long before you've got to be back on stage? Eight minutes? Do you want to miss your entry now? Because it's the last you'll be making. Hietanen takes over his rôle after the interval.'

The effect of his words on Peik was instantaneous: every trace of frenzy and hysteria drained from him, leaving him as rigid as his still silent rival: he stared disbelievingly at Andrei while faintly in the distance there could be heard the voice of Donna Anna inciting Don Ottavio to vengeance and his equivocating replies. Then with every trace of emotion under control Peik turned full-face towards Andrei.

'No!' he said.

Andrei regarded him without expression. 'You have nothing to say in the matter,' he said icily. 'Hannu Hietanen takes over his part.'

'And the audience? Do they get an explanation?'

'A part of the truth—that Hannu was assaulted by an unknown person, had difficulty in getting here but is now in a fit condition to take over his part. The announcement will precede the second act, after which we shall have no further need of you.'

Another entry, this time by Eeva, prevented any further reaction. She surged in, saw her husband and addressed him. 'I was told you were here. Just to remind you you're on again in four minutes.'

He ignored her, concentrating on his antagonists before him. 'All right,' he said quietly, 'and as soon as I leave here, as soon as I've changed, I'll find the nearest telephone and tell the police exactly where they can locate a certain lady who entered this country illegally. Nobody else at home at the Turunens' house, is there, and no telephone in the sauna, so she'll be sitting waiting to receive the police when they get there. If there should be a hitch, of course, there'll be an identity check of everyone leaving the country. I don't think there'll be any need, though.'

There was a moment of stupefied silence while Andrei and Ilmari exchanged glances. It was Ilmari who spoke.

'The police would have no interest in the matter. Go ahead and—' He broke off as Andrei seized his arm and spoke urgently and imploringly in Russian while Ilmari tried to soothe him. Finally Ilmari turned again to Peik.

'And if you're allowed to continue?'

'A matter for further discussion. Certain information about me to be withheld by one of you from the police, of course. And by the end of the performance you'll have had time to have made other arrangements, naturally.'

In full operatic fury Eeva turned on him. 'Are you blackmailing us?'

'Yes,' Peik answered her, with the impatient gesture of brushing away an irritating fly.

'Thank you,' Eeva said composedly, 'that's all I need. Look at me now: look at me on the stage if you want to, because after the end of this performance, you won't be seeing me, or my money, ever again.'

He took a step towards her and slapped her hard across the face, just as Risto appeared in considerable agitation to fetch Peik for an immediate entry. A red mark glowed on

Eeva's cheek as he seized each wrist and spat out at her, 'Strumpet!' with a glare at Risto, hesitating in the doorway to rush forward and protect her. With an even more vicious slap across her other cheek, he pushed Risto aside, turned for a second to shout 'Remember' to all in the room and raced for the stage a moment after Leporello had completed his own entry recitative and in the nick of time to approve his servant's plans for the night's orgy of eating, drinking and seduction.

An even more theatrical tableau would have been revealed to the audience if they could have seen inside the office. For ten seconds nobody stirred, rooted it seemed by the intense and varied emotions expressed by each face. Risto's face showed a blending of fury and anguish as he gazed at Eeva. She herself was apparently petrified by a combination of amazement, fury and misery. Hannu registered incomprehension and disgust, Ilmari grave foreboding, while Andrei after five seconds sank down on his chair with elbows hard on the table supporting his forehead on his fists, and with an expression of blank despair.

It was Hannu, by now the least dazed, who broke the spell. 'Can anyone please tell me what the hell all this is about?' he demanded.

Ilmari bent and whispered in Andrei's ear in Russian, was answered in that language and faced the others.

'We've known each other for some time,' he said in Finnish, 'and I believe we can trust one another, I'm going to tell you something that if it were repeated to anyone outside this room might well land Andrei and his wife in jail for a very long time. Can I trust you all to hear this and then forget it completely for at any rate the next few weeks?'

Three heads nodded assent and three spoken commitments were given. Ilmari continued, 'Briefly it concerns the escape of Andrei's wife and her presence at the moment here in Finland. Peik has discovered this and, as you heard, is making full use of it.' He looked across at Hannu apologetically and added, 'Andrei's been told that she'll be handed back if discovered and I can't convince him otherwise. So there's nothing we can do.'

'Short of arranging a convenient accident.' Hannu appeared to be meditating the feasibility of putting that idea into speedy effect.

Risto had moved forward to Anna's side, taking up the protective position of a Don Ottavio, about to give assurance and do nothing. He touched her cheek with an infinitely gentle fingertip and asked, 'How is it?'

She ignored the question. 'If there's to be any concerted plan for a murder,' she offered, 'put me in charge. I can suggest some highly efficient methods.'

For once Risto stepped out of his rôle. 'Leave it to me,' he suggested, with a grimness that transformed him. 'I can think up something. And tonight, before he can do any more harm.'

Andrei had returned to reality and entered the ghoulish discussion with what from the sound of it was a particularly virulent Russian oath. 'Give over this childishness,' he said, 'or at least postpone your arrangements till the end of the performance. He'll get it one day, that's certain. For the moment, let's get down to practical matters. Hannu, did you meet anyone at all as you came in?'

'Naturally, I couldn't avoid it. People inspecting tickets, people behind the scenes here. I don't think they noticed me much, though.'

'Are you willing to stand down this evening? You'll get your normal remuneration of course, and there'll be plenty of future opportunities for you. I'll see to that if I can.'

'It seems I have to in the circumstances.'

'Good. I'll see that it gets round that you've arrived after an accident and I've decided you're not fit enough to take over. We'll find somewhere for you to lock yourself in so that nobody knows you're around. The audience will have to think you haven't turned up. It seems to me that the less attention you attract by actually leaving now, the better. I know somewhere reasonably comfortable where you can wait and one of us will bring you whatever you want from the café. You're probably hungry.'

'I'm not really feeling too good anyhow,' Hannu admitted, 'otherwise I might make more fuss.'

As a true professional, whatever his private emotions, Risto was aware of the course of the action on the stage. 'We've got only a few more minutes,' he said to Eeva. 'Are you well enough to carry on?'

'Of course,' she responded scornfully. 'The mask will hide part of my face anyhow.' Absorbed in their own preoccupations they left the room.

It was Ilmari who assured himself the coast was clear and, taking a key with him, led Hannu up narrow stone steps spiralling between walls to a room above, where he left him in reasonable comfort. Later he returned with soup, sandwiches and two bottles of beer. During the interval, having changed into everyday clothes, he made his way unrecognized to the auditorium where he found the Turunens on their way to the buffet. He had a hurried word with Ritva and Markku, who with their children made their way to the exit and their car parked on the main island. Ilmari returned to his dressing-room where he sat meditating for a long time before starting preparations for his appearance as the avenging Statue.

During the interval Peik disappeared into the dressing-room, locking the door behind him, and when he reappeared for the Second Act it was clear that he had been drinking. His former tense excitement was subsiding and his movements were more uncertain and slower. At the same time, under its make-up his face was ashen white and appeared shrunken and he was having problems in focusing his eyes. His return to the stage served for some time to reanimate him so that his opening protest to a scared Leporello, determined to cut loose from this madman, had much of the appropriate mocking detachment which he managed to maintain through the serenade. His performance was flagging during the encounters with Masetto, the villagers and the unfortunate Donna Elvira, though not too noticeably: the presentation as a whole was so excellent that most of the audience were enthralled by acting, singing and staging without being much aware of individual weaknesses and uncertainty. It was when he was addressing the statue of his victim, the Commendatore, issuing the rash invitation to supper, that a very real deterioration was apparent. He seemed to be having difficulty in standing: he missed an entry and then another, ignoring the words lost to plunge in wildly and late, even on occasion singing flat. He was an almost pathetic figure, giving the impression of clutching at the notes rather than singing with the unchallengeable confidence of the wealthy, greedy, dissolute aristocrat, supremely sure of himself whatever Hell might have prepared for him. It was only with the entrance of the Statue in the midst of the banquet that he appeared to rouse himself, though to the more sensitive of his audience his defiance of his ghostly visitor seemed to have taken on a personal note: it was Peik Arvika himself mocking his doom, yelling defiance at the universe. Again and again he rejected repentance, the deep bass demand—'*Si*' evoking an increasingly savage '*No*', until the final pronouncement of the Statue that his time was up was followed by appalling shrieks from the Punished Libertine (an earlier name for the work) as he felt the first torments, still gripped by the mailed hand of the Statue dragging him down to Hell.

Entranced by the sheer power of plot, acting and music, the audience relaxed to the angry cries of characters storming in, intent on their own minor reprisals and met with Leporello's shocked account of his master's prior disposal. Ottavio, seeking his reward from Anna, accepted her request for a year of mourning; Elvira was to retire to a convent; Masetto and Zerlina were well on their way to a reconciliation, while Leporello set off for a tavern and a new master, tiny ripples of human concern to round off hastily the horrifying doom of the figure in whose orbit they had been puppet-dancing. Nobody had a thought to spare for the hypnotic puppet-master who had manipulated all of them though everyone finally agreed that:

> This is the end of those who do evil,
> And in this life the wrongdoers
> Always get their just deserts.

This was the point at which the second hitch of the evening occurred: one principal had failed to turn up for the opening curtain; the other was absent for the final one. When all had assembled for the bowing and speeches, Peik Arvika, on whom the main spotlight should have focused, was not among them. It was in fact only at the last moment before the curtain-call that it was realized that Giovanni might well be anywhere (not excluding his apparent destination, the infernal regions), the only exception being the place he was supposed to be.

There was an immediate and frantic search which concentrated on the area around the Suvorov Channel (in the region of which he should have emerged from the stage), on corridors, café and dressing-rooms and on anywhere backstage that the searchers could think of, though there was little time for more than a hurried glance round. From the audience came increasing sounds of restlessness, some of them already slipping away. Andrei was forced into making impromptu changes in the normal practice of lining up the chorus and then progressing through the soloists according to their importance, with Leporello and Giovanni coming last, Leporello then departing to leave his master to receive the principal ovation. The anti-climax of a non-appearance of the eagerly-awaited principal would have been inconceivable so in these exceptional circumstances

Andrei himself appeared on an empty stage. He held up his hand, delaying those making their exit and hushing all sound, thus giving due weight and impressiveness to his English words.

'It is with the deepest regret that I have to inform you that Peik Arvika, whom at this moment you should have been applauding for a great performance, cannot be here to respond to that applause. You may have been aware during the Second Act that he was evidently ill, suffering indeed from one of the violent headaches that have been plaguing him recently. On completing his rôle, he collapsed and is now unconscious. I feel this is not a moment for congratulations, much as you may have wished to express it, and accordingly the performers would all prefer not to appear and invite it. We can only hope that you have enjoyed what you have seen and will be here again next year when we should like to have Peik back with us, fully restored to health. I wish you all good night.'

The stage manager was ready with a Finnish translation. A few of the audience responded to these formal announcements by automatically starting to clap but this was stilled immediately they realized its inappropriateness and a sober and thoughtful procession eventually made its way across the two bridges.

Ilmari would apparently have been the last person to see Peik and Andrei at once turned to him to ask about the direction he had taken on leaving the stage. According to Ilmari, he had asked Peik how he felt: Peik had ignored him and had staggered towards the open space by the Suvorov Channel, turning once to tell Ilmari he needed a moment to himself: he'd be in time for the curtain calls. Ilmari had waited uncertain for a couple of minutes and had then gone into this area to discover whether all was well; seeing no one there, he had assumed that Peik had gone back some other way so had returned himself only just in time. Nobody else could give any information and the search was resumed.

A visit to his dressing-room revealed that he must have changed and taken his costume somewhere with him: both everyday suit and dark green costume were missing. Several of the performers were already removing make-up and changing, as they hoped to return to their own homes the same evening, the usual final get-together having taken place the evening before. Without the least intention of ever setting eyes on her husband again, Eeva had accepted the hospitality of Kaarina at Joensuu for the night and her help and support if need be in clearing her possessions later from the villa she and Peik had occupied. Hannu had already slipped away from his self-imprisonment though nobody knew when, and Risto, looking like a ghost, had almost pestered Eeva with offers of help and words of comfort before taking himself off.

Andrei continued the search for the comparatively short time it took Ilmari to change. The two men were joined by the comrade waiting at the castle gate, inordinately worried in case his charge had somehow managed to evade him by swimming or rowing across the water, and together they crossed the bridges. Guardian and ward walked together to their hotel through the gathering dusk while Ilmari easily located his car in the parking area. He set out for Lahti and home.

As Andrei and his comrade made their way along the main street they were passed by an unrecognized motor-caravan driven by Markku Turunen and having within its cramped but adequate interior four more people: his wife, his two children and a middle-aged lady who spoke no Finnish but only English and Russian. She had been spending the past twenty-four hours with them, though she had kept exclus-ively to their sauna building. Markku and Ritva took turns in driving through the night towards Naantali on the west coast. Some way before they reached it, they stopped to eat breakfast and as they approached the harbour area their guest took refuge on a top bunk with various bags and parcels arranged along its outer edge. There was no passport check or inspection, however, and they drove serenely on to the Swedish-registered ferry bound for Kapellskär. Once the boat was under way the family went off to explore its possibilities but the middle-aged lady seemed to prefer her secluded isolation. It was only after they had left the boat and were on their way to visit Uppsala before turning south for their final destination, Stockholm, that she showed much interest in her surroundings, staring with wonder and also suspicion at the comfortable farmhouses, family houses and shining blocks of flats.

But she asked only one question: 'Do you really think he can make the journey safely?'

6. VERY FAR FROM HOME

Tatiana Oblodskaya had just missed her bus and had decided she might as well walk the kilometre or so to her flat in the suburbs of Viipuri. The heatwave had continued for the past fortnight—well over thirty degrees today—and as she plodded through the small park, a heavy shopping-bag in each hand, she decided on a half-way rest on one of the park benches shaded by a group of sycamore trees. After all, though now over seventy and provided with a reasonable State pension, she still did a fair number of private cleaning jobs for women at work all day: this morning she'd already been working for two hours before going shopping. She often stopped here, and had her favourite seat, near enough to the road but secluded and shaded by trees and rarely used.

Today, however, it was occupied by another woman, younger than Tatiana and apparently asleep. Tatiana lowered her solidly-built body on to the far end of the seat, leaned back and breathed a sigh of relief. It was good to be away from people for a bit even though she was near enough

to the road for the noise of the traffic to be disturbing. It
didn't matter much: you couldn't get away from noise of
some kind and it was pleasant to be able to look up through
the leaves at the milky-white sky.

Her eyes turned towards the woman a short way from
her. There was something odd about her. She didn't seem
to be Russian. It wasn't her clothing: her blue dress was
ordinary enough: it was something about the build, the
features and structure of the face. More like one of these
Western tourists you saw arriving in their coaches in the
town centre, though hardly one of the Finns. They had
plenty of their own Finns, or rather Finnish Russians, living
here in Eastern Karelia and still speaking their strange
language, but this woman was certainly not one of them.
And she was in such an odd position: slumped on the seat,
almost as if she'd been thrown there, and her head was
lolling forward on her chest. She was breathing heavily,
with an occasional gasp for air, and her face was a peculiar
chalky colour.

Slightly alarmed, Tatiana moved alongside her unknown
companion and shook her by the shoulder. The woman
moaned faintly but made no intelligible response. Not drunk
anyhow: there was no trace of alcohol on her breath. She
must be ill, Tatiana thought. Surely a woman of her age, at
least forty, wouldn't be under the influence of one of those
drugs that so many Westerners depend on.

She caught sight of an elderly man, one of her neighbours,
walking vigorously along the path beyond the trees and
called to him. 'Comrade,' she shouted, never having learned
his name, 'could you spare a minute?'

The man turned his head in surprise and came through
the trees towards her. 'Good morning, Comrade Oblodskaya,' he said, it being his duty to be acquainted with his
neighbours' names and possibly other things as well,
'What's the matter?' He had already caught sight of the
sleeping woman.

'She seems to be ill, or worse,' Tatiana reported. 'I tried
to wake her but she only moaned. And I ought to be on my
way home: I've got a meal to prepare.'

'Can't do that,' the man said. 'This woman needs attention. I don't like the look of her. And the police will have to
be informed.'

Just what I was afraid of, Tatiana thought to herself, but
she limited herself to saying aloud, 'How? There aren't any
police around here.'

There was indeed no sign of a policeman in this quiet
park. But the man took his civic responsibilities seriously.
'There's a café just the other side of the street. I'll phone
from there.'

He trotted off briskly, leaving Tatiana framing in her
mind all the things she would have liked to be able to tell
him to do with himself for insisting on dragging her into
what could only spell trouble and at the least be a stupid
waste of time.

But it was an ambulance that came some ten minutes
later. The man not having noticed and therefore reported
the woman's unusual appearance, had assumed that she
was either ill or drunk. She was deposited on a stretcher,
transported into the ambulance and delivered to the town
hospital.

So it was in a hospital ward that Iris regained conscious-
ness, as indeed had been intended. She stirred restlessly for
a few moments and then her eyes focused on the unsym-
pathetic face of a nurse, who addressed her in an incomprehensible language. Iris gazed at her in muddled bewilderment before asking in English the only possible question in
the circumstances, 'Where am I?'

The words, simple and clear enough it would seem,
appeared to have a curious effect. The nurse looked slightly
alarmed, regarded Iris more closely and again produced a
quite incomprehensible sentence. Iris burst into tears.

With the impatient sigh that nurses world-wide reserve

for fractious and over-emotional patients, the woman stalked off, returning a few minutes later with another nurse, clearly of greater age and authority, who produced at first equally strange sounds and later incomprehensible words that sounded like Finnish. Transported seemingly to some other planet, but by now slightly more adjusted to her surroundings, Iris gulped, 'English. English. Not understand. Speak English.'

While it may be a myth to claim that nothing can put any nurse out of her stride, this generalization certainly does apply to hospital sisters everywhere. The older nurse, with the tight mouth that had never extended into a smile, gave her junior crisp directions which sent her scurrying off, while she herself stood regarding Iris silently and with intense disapproval.

Ten minutes later the nurse reappeared with a small, nervous-looking man in a white overall. He tried first to communicate in his own language, with no success, and then, obviously grasping at straws of memory, brought out:

'Speak you in English?'

'I am English,' Iris whispered, tears still trickling down her cheeks.

The man paused, uncertain of the next step, and then produced:

'Are you of Vyborg?'

'I am from London, England.' Though the world seemed to be revolving around her, Iris sounded quite sure about this at least.

The man looked even more depressed and uncertain.

'They say they find no papers,' he informed her.

'What papers?' She was having difficulty in controlling her voice which wobbled about.

'Documents. Who you are,' and, clearly a sudden inspiration, 'passports.'

'I don't know,' Iris wobbled unhelpfully, and, returning to basics, asked plaintively again, 'Where am I?'

The man paused, considering whether his coming disclosure might be construed later as giving away secret information, decided he might risk it and replied, 'You are in hospital of Vyborg, in Soviet Union.'

Something was stirring uncertainly in Iris's memory. 'Oh,' she responded with suitable vagueness. One thing was certain: she must have ten minutes to pull herself together, reactivate her brain to make sense of all this.

'I'm thirsty,' she said pleadingly, lifting a non-existent glass to her mouth and promptly bursting into tears again.

She managed to stop crying to drink the water and while she was doing this, a conference got under way at the foot of her bed between the man in the overall, the sister and various other people who had materialized. Finally the man informed her,

'You must speak with the police.'

'Oh,' she said a second time, and promptly sank back on the pillow and closed her eyes, breathing heavily as if asleep or again unconscious.

In fact she was sufficiently conscious now to experience a number of sensations, none of them pleasant. There was a helpless weakness, a floating, almost dissolving feeling, the near-certainty that she would soon be sick, a deep foreboding, almost panic, and indeed an overwhelming sleepiness which she fought against. She had to concentrate, to gather together the wisps of ideas that were floating in her mind, to remember, remember and prepare.

Half an hour later she was aroused, given a plate of thick soup to drink and as soon as she had finished it, helped out of bed and into a brown dressing-gown and slippers. It was only then that she realized she had been put into some kind of hospital nightdress. She was led by the arm to a small room at the far end of the corridor adjoining the ward. At a table inside, a man and woman were awaiting her. Neither was in uniform but Iris, whose head had cleared considerably during the past half-hour, had no doubt whatever that they were at least connected with the police.

It was a three-sided conversation, the man asking the questions in Russian, the woman translating with reasonable efficiency and Iris answering in English. The atmosphere had something of the formality and neutrality of a job interview: no expression showed on the interviewers' faces and no feeling or attitude—hostility, impatience or disbelief —appeared in their questions.

These concerned first her name, nationality, where she lived and what she did there, how she had come to Russia and what she had been doing there. Iris answered vaguely but willingly before herself breaking into a number of questions of her own.

'Can you please tell me where I am?' she asked, looking thoroughly frightened. 'I don't understand. What am I doing here? What's happened to me?'

The man and the woman spoke together for a few moments and the woman turned to Iris. 'You're in Vyborg in Soviet Union and we try to find out how you came here. Don't you remember? How did you come and how long have you been here?'

By now Iris had managed to recollect all this pretty clearly but she spoke falteringly. 'I came in a bus from somewhere: it was a Finnish bus I remember. We stopped somewhere and I remember getting out, but I don't know when it was.'

'Did you come here from Finland?'

Iris frowned in concentration and then ventured, 'Yes, it was Finland. I was on holiday there: I'd come from England. I was travelling to places by train, I remember that.' She was speaking slowly, recollecting with obvious difficulty. 'I was on that bus but I don't remember why.'

The man was scribbling notes as the woman translated. Then the woman asked, 'Were you travelling alone?'

'Oh yes. I usually travel alone. I like to go where I want to and change my mind. Yes, I remember. I was in a Finnish town but I don't remember the name now and I saw a

tourist booklet about Russia and they told me about a bus
trip to Leningrad. I had still got about two weeks and I
made a booking because I wanted to see Russia.'

'Is this your first visit?'

'Yes, it is. But what happened to me?' There was mount-
ing concern in her voice. 'And where are all my things: my
handbag and my case? Where are they?'

'We'll see about them,' the woman said, almost comfort-
ingly. 'Now tell us what happened when you got out of the
bus. Why did you get out? Did the other people get out too?
Were you going to visit somewhere?'

'There were a lot of people getting out,' Iris said slowly.
'They went somewhere but I didn't go with them. I crossed
the street but I don't remember why.'

'Did you speak to anybody?'

Iris was looking down at her hands which were moving
restlessly on her lap. She again seemed on the verge of tears.
'Yes,' she said, 'there was a woman. She dropped her keys
and I picked them up for her. She said something to me in
Russian and then when I didn't understand, she spoke in
English. She said her flat was just along the street: would I
like to see it? I think I said "yes" but after that I don't
remember anything.'

'What was the woman like?'

'I didn't notice except she seemed older, like an ordinary
housewife and she spoke English badly. But she wouldn't
have stolen my handbag: I'm sure she wasn't that kind of
person. Oh, I do feel ill. My arm hurts too, just here.' She
touched the upper part of her arm just above the elbow.

There was a longer conversation between the two and the
man finally nodded approval. The woman said, 'You had
an injection there. Don't you remember that, even?' Iris
shook her head again helplessly while she searched desper-
ately for a handkerchief in the non-existent pockets of the
dressing-gown.

There was clearly nothing more to be got out of her at

present except the name of the place the coach was going
to. The woman recited a list of towns from which coaches
travelled: Helsinki, Tampere, Vaasa, Jyväskylä, Turku,
Kuopio: Iris recognized the first two and the last two,
having visited them, but Mikkeli being an intermediate
point and not a terminus was not mentioned. She finally
subdued her tears to say she thought the place had begun
with an M, but she couldn't remember any more: she
didn't speak Finnish. All this evoked no immediate response.
Finally as she seemed unable to tell them any more, she was
returned to bed and inquiries were carried out elsewhere.

Full-scale investigations now got under way. A call went
through to Passport Control, from where the officials inspecting passports at each end of the control zone had to be
located. Both of them remembered a British passport
handed over by a nondescript woman, who appeared to
correspond to the photographs in passport and visa. The
bus in question, one of six that afternoon, was on its way to
Kuopio. The Finnish officials when contacted remembered
checking the passport in the office: in the six buses there
had been two West Germans, three British and a Swede
and the officials were slightly vague about which bus the
woman in question had been travelling on: the man who
had actually boarded some of the buses was off duty that
day. They would continue their inquiries.

Inquiries of the Soviet Embassy in Helsinki gathered
information about the visa issued. The copy available there
showed the name as Ramona Iris Lawton, who was described as a teacher and the relevant passport had been
issued in London three years previously. A telecopy of the
photograph sent to Viipuri was shown to the hospital staff
and was attested to as resembling the woman being held
there.

The Finnish state police were naturally requested to
help with the investigation. Was there any information to
substantiate the woman's claim that she had only recently

entered Finland? Visits to airline and shipping agencies revealed eventually that a Miss Lawton had travelled from Germany on the Travemünde–Helsinki line a fortnight before. It took two or three days to trace her route across Finland by means of hotel registers: she had stayed overnight in Lahti, Mikkeli, Joensuu, Kuopio, Jyväskylä and Tampere before returning to Helsinki for a few days. Records ended the night before the departure of the bus to Leningrad.

The police also questioned the Finnish guide who had accompanied the coach but he could tell them little that was helpful. He spoke some English and had given her all the essential information about times and arrangements in that language but otherwise she had seemed reserved and had made no attempt to start a conversation with him. He'd noticed though that the woman next to her in the coach had done some interpreting for her. He was sure the two women had not come together: in fact each was sharing a hotel-room with a different woman. The seat companion had mentioned she was working in Stockholm and would be going straight back there immediately on their return to Finland. The driver could not be located yet as he was already off on another tour to Norway: he apparently spoke no English and was unlikely to have had any contact with her.

Other enquiries were being carried out locally. Every flat in an area that covered a ten-minute walk from the station was visited and the residents questioned. The bus was reported to have arrived at about half past two and the police were instructed to discover anyone who had been either in the nearby streets or looking out of a window at around that time. Results at first were meagre. Several people had been in the street but only one man had noticed a woman stoop to pick something up and hand it to a second woman. They had talked for a bit as he came towards them and then the two of them had passed him though by that time they had crossed to the other side of the street. He hadn't noticed anything much about them: middle-aged and ordinary: he had no recollection even of what they had been wearing. Now, if they'd been twenty years younger . . .

Special attention was given to homes in the area the two might have been making their way towards, assuming Iris's story to be true, and it was in one of the flats the police visited that a shred of information came to light. An elderly woman, unfortunately not with the best eyesight, who had been sitting with her knitting at her fourth-floor window overlooking a courtyard, had noticed two women come into the yard and approach a car standing there, as if they were on their way to the house door beyond it. She hadn't been able to see them very closely but she was able to say that both had been middle-aged and about the same height: one was wearing a blue dress and the other a fawn coat. When they were quite near the car, a man had got out of it: he was dark-haired but she hadn't seen much more as he was partly hidden by another car next to his. The woman in blue obviously knew him and she'd introduced him to the woman in the fawn coat: they'd shaken hands. Then she'd had the impression that the woman in the coat had been forced into the car and the other two had got in very quickly at front and back. The car had reversed almost immediately and driven quickly out of the yard, turning right into the street. It had been black and ordinary: she knew nothing about the different makes. She hadn't reported anything as she wasn't at all sure about what she'd seen, especially with the other car alongside and she could have imagined it: everything had happened so quickly.

Nobody else had seen anything, most people being at work at that time of day, their children at summer camps and several families on holiday elsewhere.

It seemed there was at least an element of truth in Iris's story: there had been another woman involved and now it seemed, a man. Robbery could have been the motive for the drugging, the stealing not so much of money but of a passport that might ensure a passage out of the country.

Many questions remained unsolved even so. The most important, naturally, was the identity of the woman defector, if indeed she was one. All they knew at present was that she must have had some resemblance to Miss Lawton. Had their meeting been planned in advance or had the couple been waiting for a suitable victim, someone walking alone and of not dissimilar appearance, and taken this opportunity? They might have been waiting for some time, observing the occupants of the various Finnish buses that stopped here. Some of the tourists might want to have a last-minute visit to the hard-currency tourist shop quite near where the meeting apparently took place. Further interrogation of Miss Lawton might extract something useful though, having nothing definite against her, they would have to soft-pedal a bit.

Iris was now living in isolation in a small room in the hospital with a policeman outside the door: in the circumstances this had seemed the wisest course. She had also had her clothes returned and in her plain short-sleeved dress, her face pale and woebegone, her hair limp and bedraggled as nobody had thought to provide her with a comb, she looked considerably older than the age on her visa. She had clearly recovered fully from the effects of the drug but she was now beginning to show impatience as the questioning got under way. This time she was facing two older men in uniform and a highly-efficient but somewhat hectoring woman interpreter of her own age.

The same ground was covered but with more attention to what she'd been doing during the past year. With growing resentment, she described her teaching in North-West London, the mother she'd visited in Winchester at weekends, and her decision to visit Finland: friends of hers had toured the country in their car the previous year and had praised it highly. When the questioning passed to her recent experience in Viipuri, Iris had now recalled that the woman sitting next to her had told her they had half an hour to change

roubles in the station. Iris had crossed the road with the
idea of seeing something of the town in the time available
and had then picked up the woman's keys. She now remembered too going into a courtyard with the woman and being
introduced to a man there, but could recall nothing after
that.

The questions continued, mostly repetition of earlier questions, till finally Iris lost the last of her patience. Gripping
the sides of her hard chair and sitting bolt upright, she
demanded:

'Why are you asking all these questions as if I was a
criminal? I come to your country as a tourist and am
drugged, it seems, and have all my money and my passport
stolen and instead of looking for the criminals and getting
my things back for me, you keep questioning me as if it was
all my fault. I demand to have the British consul here.'

'I don't think you're being quite frank with us, Miss
Lawton,' the woman interpreted. 'Now, what was your real
reason for visiting Russia?'

'It's just what you read in the papers,' Iris retorted
furiously. 'Some of my friends said that if I came here I
wouldn't get out again. I just said they were joking. Do you
think I'm a spy or something? I've told you everything I
can, and if this is a civilized country you'll arrange with the
British consul for me to be sent home. And now I insist on
speaking to him on the telephone if he can't come here.'

'The consul will come later when he's free. But we'd like
some more information from you first.'

'And if I can't give any more, because I've already told
you all I know, you'll start torturing me and give me truth
drugs and do all the other things I've never really believed
till now. Well my mother in England knows I'm here and
I'd promised to phone her as soon as I got back to Finland.
She'll be worried out of her mind. And she'll have got into
touch with our MP, our Member of Parliament, though you
probably haven't got any here, and the police and the

Foreign Office too and then there'll be trouble.'

She sat there scowling at them, hoping she wasn't over-playing her part, wondering how the teacher she was de-scribed as on the visa would have reacted. If she had indeed been as innocent as she pretended she would of course have known, but they themselves would hardly know what to expect from a teacher, especially a foreign one. They con-tinued to question her, at times deliberately framing a question as a bait to get her talking, but she merely sat there, her lips pressed tightly together, her face as blank and defiant as she could make it. Eventually she was conduc-ted back to her room, her padded cell as she had christened it—any form of padding being noticeably absent—and locked in. She curled up on the rock-hard bed and contem-plated the single bare wooden chair that was the only furniture.

It was at nine o'clock the following morning that a report from the Helsinki Embassy reached the Foreign Office in Moscow that Dr Andrei Pavlov, due back in Leningrad that day, had disappeared. He had insisted on staying a further day in Finland to clear up matters in the theatre in Savon-linna. An additional comrade had been dispatched from the Embassy and had installed himself in the hotel reception lounge under the uneasy eye of the night porter. The doctor had retired early to his hotel room with his faithful first comrade in the adjoining one, but the following morning the bird was found to have flown. Soon after retiring, the doctor had in fact departed down the back stairs and through the door into the car park where Ilmari had been waiting for him in his car. The journey to the Tornio-Haparanda frontier had taken some seven hours and they had joined the line of cars carrying Finnish workers and early-morning shoppers across the border to Sweden. Andrei had humped up the blankets on his bed in the hotel just in case his companion should glance in to check that he was there and it seemed unlikely that any alarm had been given yet.

And for greater assurance Ilmari had piled some camping equipment on the back seat which hid sufficiently well the large man crouched on the floor beneath it.

The KGB chewed over this unwelcome news for some time before ordering the defector's wife to be brought in for questioning, but further delay ensued when neighbours informed him she had been called to her brother's bedside in Leningrad a few days before. A search there was suspended late in the afternoon when a news flash picked up from Sweden announced that the Soviet opera director had arrived that morning by plane from the north of the country to be met at the airport by his wife Natasha who had arrived secretly the day before. Both were requesting political asylum. The news report recalled how Dr Pavlov's contract to produce an opera in Stockholm had been cancelled by the Russians a few weeks previously 'on account of other commitments'.

This was not the first disturbing radio broadcast of the day. Early in the morning both the BBC World Service and their domestic news bulletins had been referring to a report that a middle-aged British woman teacher who had departed from Finland on a coach tour to Leningrad had apparently not returned from her visit. She had failed to telephone her seventy-year-old mother two days before as she had promised to do on arriving back in Finland and had also failed to claim her plane reservation to Heathrow the following day. The coach courier, when interviewed by a British correspondent flown in from Helsinki, had said he'd already been questioned about her by the Finnish police at the request of the Soviet authorities: apparently she was being detained in Russia for interrogation. He had not been aware she was missing as it was now clear that some other woman of similar appearance had taken her place and had been undetected in all frontier identity checks.

Urgent inquiries about the whereabouts of the British woman were made to the Soviet authorities by the British

Embassy in Moscow, but these were met by an automatic denial of all knowledge of such a person. Lunch-time British television programmes showed pictures of a frail-looking mother and a ten-year-old photograph of a slightly recognizable Iris standing with a class of children in a school where she had once spent a summer as a supply teacher. Both photographs had been selected to be used on this occasion by Iris herself during her recent visit to her mother.

The morning popular press had been published too early to take advantage of this heart-rending tale but greater drama was afforded them in the early evening of the same day. In Stockholm, Natasha Pavlov, wife of the world-famous opera producer who had just claimed asylum there, had asked for a statement to be made public. It concerned her recent escape from the Soviet Union and referred to a male collaborator she had had there, who had been responsible for ensuring her escape. He had suggested the idea of a substitute among the Finnish coach tourists who usually spent a short time in Viipuri to change money and maybe have a last look round on their return journey to Finland. Natasha would try to look as ordinary as possible and it shouldn't be too difficult to find someone sufficiently like her among the thousand or so Finns who passed through each week. In fact there might well be several possibilities. If one of these were to cross the road to the hard-currency tourist shop, Natasha and her accomplice would try to find a means of separating her from the others, abducting and incapacitating her by some means and thus get hold of her handbag, which would almost certainly contain her passport and visa. Twice before the man had inspected the Leningrad-bound coaches but the few women who might have suited had all been accompanied by husband or friends. On this occasion he'd spotted a woman who was alone and who could have passed for Natasha, so he'd found a pretext for bringing Natasha to Leningrad and from there to Viipuri shortly before the arrival of the coaches on their return journey. Their plan had worked: the woman had been seized and her handbag stolen and she had been kept under drugs and left on a bench in a local park the following morning where she would soon be discovered. Having been told about the BBC news broadcasts, Mrs Pavlov was now extremely upset to think the woman might be in trouble on her account: she'd had nothing whatever to do with Mrs Pavlov's escape.

By this time, by means of his own, the British consul in Leningrad had located Iris and insisted on seeing her. She looked decidedly limp and dishevelled, having asked in vain for a comb—strangely enough for a resident in a hospital, no toothbrush had been forthcoming either: she had washed in a bathroom with unmistakably Russian soap and dried herself on a not overclean roller towel. The fastidious consul with a fashion-model wife had wondered about the dreary types who got themselves into trouble in foreign lands where they were completely out of their depth. However, he listened patiently to her story, decided she hadn't the intelligence to have made it up, and reported her back to London as just another silly woman—exactly as Iris had intended.

Appeals, discussions, directives, denials which soon changed to indignant affirmation, charges of illegal interference in the affairs of a sovereign state, of assistance given to and involvement in subversive activities: counter-charges of attempts to prejudice the development of amicable trade and economic understanding between two nations whose potential cooperation in these fields could be of the maximum benefit to each—the message was clear enough. With their considerable intelligence and knowledge of the world, the officials of the KGB had no doubt whatsoever of Iris's active involvement: Mrs Pavlov's exculpation with all its implausibility and obvious invention had made them all the more certain. But they had no shred of solid evidence to advance in what would have had to be a public trial and, in view of impending diplomatic and trade exchanges, there was nothing to gain by prolonging the agony and incidentally creating a bogey image for the more nervous among potential tourists.

So ten days later Iris was put aboard an Ilyushin bound for Heathrow, still wearing her blue dress on a decidedly chilly and windy day. She was received on landing by two Foreign Office personnel who questioned her at length, though mainly, Iris was thankful to discover, about her experiences in the Soviet Union rather than those of the period preceding her visit. They seemed reasonably satisfied with her replies and very kindly suggested how she could leave the airport building by a route that avoided the waiting journalists. She sought refuge for the next few days with a cousin in London while her mother dealt with the phone calls.

She felt extremely tired, but in a way triumphant: in repeating her story she'd realized its thinness, but, probably through no merit of her own, she'd survived. Adventure had to have its worrying moments. It was only a week later that she remembered Ilmari. She tried his telephone number but the telephone seemed to have been disconnected: maybe the result of the storm damage, she thought. Probably he had telephoned her mother's number and had been discouraged as an unwelcome news reporter. She felt sad and yet relieved: he might indeed have hypnotized her into marriage and a quiet life in his village as a vet's wife. And then what about all the other places in the world that were still waiting to be discovered? She turned her full attention to the problem of getting a new job—somewhere overseas of course.

INTERLUDE

HELL IS A COLD WET PLACE

August brought with it a change in the weather. Blue lakes darkened to changing shades of grey as huge massed clouds surged over them, and a few days later rain set in persistently, though not heavily. After a week or so the wind veered to the north-west, sweeping away the rain but maintaining an unrelieved greyness. Farmers regarded sodden corn with little hope and families in unheated summer cottages scurried back a fortnight before they had intended to double-glazed flats in town.

A further change in wind direction in early September produced howling gales which uprooted trees, halted boat services on the lakes and caused the final devastation of any late crops the farmers might have hoped for. As the gales moderated slightly, the rain started in earnest, lashing forest and field, lake and human habitation. Rivers flooded over vast areas, depositing far and wide mud and debris and hundreds of logs floating on their way south to the timber-yards and pulp factories. Lakes invaded their shores, flooding sauna huts, summer cottages on their banks and town houses and blocks of flats, whose owners cherished the view of distant water but did not appreciate the sight of it swirling in cellars and kitchens.

Sheltered though it was, the Suvorov Channel rose by several centimetres, building up pressure against the grille at its southern end. And a dark shape that had been jammed under it was forced forward into the lake, moved rapidly eastward round the island on which the castle stood and came to rest on the shore of a nearby cape abandoned by the campers who had made it their summer home. For several days it lay there, sinking slightly into a glutinous churned-up mud-swamp, until a belated return of summer dried and hardened the earth sufficiently for an inspection for probable damage to be made. The camp-site supervisor bent to examine the almost unidentifiable object and within a minute had sent his companion to the nearest telephone in inform the police that the remains of a human body had been washed ashore. The lake waters, decidedly chilly even in high summer, had retarded decomposition and a saturated greenish-black material still clung to the corpse, with tiny flecks of gold in it glinting dimly in the sunlight.

It was this material that was in due course to establish the identity of its former wearer. No report of Peik's disappearance had been made to the police, it having been assumed that he had taken himself off somewhere, possibly abroad, where he might have had some remains of his earlier fortune stashed away in a bank. Certainly there would have been no future in Finland for anyone of his unpopularity and unsavoury reputation. After the first few days he had been forgotten: only Eeva might conceivably have wanted to locate him eventually if she were to start divorce proceedings, though at the moment she had taken refuge in a summer cottage she had rented, out of reach of friends, agents and the Press in the northern wilderness of Kainuu. It stood near a quiet sandy beach facing across the vast distances of Oulunjärvi, the Lake of Oulu, and here she could wander and imagine herself on the edge of a great sea.

Medical evidence established that the body must have been in the water for around two months. Further investigation, which took account of the direction of the current, led the police to the Suvorov Channel and shreds of material were located clinging to the underwater grille. It was now evident where death had taken place, and this, combined with medical evidence and information volunteered by members of the chorus living in Savonlinna relating to the mysterious disappearance of the singer, supported a reasonable conjecture that his death must have followed fairly closely the final performance of *Don Giovanni*.

This appalling and melodramatic end to what had formerly been an international operatic career was featured not only in all Finnish dailies and on radio and television but also in most other European countries. The most likely assumption was that of accidental death: the singer had collapsed and fallen into the water, reference being made to the deterioration in his performance and the final announcement about his collapse. The director, when interviewed in Sweden (where his assignment to produce an opera had in fact been kept open for him), admitted that his announcement had been designed to cover the unaccountable disappearance of the singer which would have been both embarrassing and difficult to explain. In fact nobody seemed to have seen him after he had left the stage, except Ilmari Karhu who had spoken to him and had been assured by him that he would be there for the curtain call. In view of the singer's declining health and reputation, there was naturally the possibility of suicide. His wife seemed to have left him though she had not yet been located, while his parents vented a tirade of loathing against the lady in question who, having made him suffer for years, had now either driven him to an untimely end or murdered him with her own hands.

It was the following day that even more sensational news reached the world's press and networks. An autopsy had shown that the distinguished Finnish baritone, Peik Arvika, had been dead already when he had entered the water: there seemed little doubt he had been murdered. Death might well have been due to strangulation from behind but it was obviously quite impossible at this stage to establish the real facts.

An open verdict was returned at the inquest but the police had already decided to continue their investigations into what could well be a case of homicide and the Criminal Investigation Department in Helsinki took charge.

ACT 2

1. A VISIT TO THE DOCTOR

Superintendent Arvo Laurila of the Finnish Criminal Police, now in his mid-thirties, was unmistakably a Finn. He was of medium height and medium build, with light straw-coloured straight hair and a rectangular pale face, lake-blue eyes and a placid but alert expression. His voice was deep and mellow and his speech had that soothing and comforting quality derived from a language with more than its fair share of prolonged rounded vowels and diphthongs.

He enjoyed music and knew a fair amount about opera, and with his excellent command of English it was decided that he was the best person to take charge of a case which might involve certain people with little acquaintance with Finnish. So the day after the 'Opera Case' (as it was referred to in the Press), he was despatched to Savonlinna to carry out some preliminary investigations at the scene of the crime even though most of those involved had by now scattered to the four winds.

His first visit was to the local police force who arranged with the Savonlinna Tourist Office for a competent guide to the Castle to be placed at his disposal. She met him at the main door to the castle armed with various surveyors' plans and spent the first ten minutes indicating on them the position of towers, bastions, the main rooms open to visitors and those that were not, the battlements and the compli- cated means of access to everything. They then set out to explore the reality, following passages, squeezing their way up and down steep spiral walled staircases, braving a chilly

wind on the battlements and concentrating most of their
attention on the stage, regions backstage, dressing-rooms,
corridors, means of access to the stage at all levels and above
all the short passage leading from stage to the Suvorov
Courtyard where the singer had last been seen alive. Arvo
paid special attention to the channel itself, now reflecting
the yellows and golds of the leaves of surrounding trees, but
decided to do without wading through the water for a look
at the confining grille at one end, a full report on that sinister
location having already been prepared and made available
by the town police.

With the *mise-en-scène* now fairly clear in his head, Arvo
was escorted to the Tourist Office itself and introduced to
its Director, a cheerful and efficient youngish man, who
provided them with brochures about the Festival, especially
those with particular reference to *Don Giovanni* and the
people associated with it.

When asked for further information about the performers
and director, however, the Director regretted that he could
not provide much useful personal information. His duties
were extremely wide and varied, being concerned with all
aspects of attracting and providing for the thousands of
visitors to the Festival and though he had met a lot of the
performers socially on odd occasions, the organization and
preparation of actual performances were in other hands.
When asked if he could recommend someone living in the
town more closely connected with the opera personnel, he
suggested the two doctors, Markku and Ritva Turunen, who
were opera enthusiasts and had often provided hospitality
and entertainment, above all for members of the *Don Giovanni*
cast.

It was Ritva Turunen who answered the telephone and
informed the Director, who had made the call, that her
husband would be working in the hospital all that afternoon
but she would be able to spare the Superintendent a short
time before four o'clock when she started a consulting

period. Their flat was near the town centre and was in a comparatively new six-floor block. It was in fact a double flat, extending across the whole of the top floor, with twice the number of rooms in it of the average three-roomed Finnish apartment.

On arrival he was greeted by a country-girl maid who showed him into a hall where he automatically removed and hung up his coat. Ritva appeared at the exact moment he was ready, shook hands, identified herself and led him into her consulting room. This was a light, soothing room with racks of pot-plants enjoying the brightness of a large window and festooning here and there the cream walls. A few pictures of the Finnish countryside in summer and in winter, all of them originals and in light-coloured frames, adorned the walls, and there were several modern but comfortable chairs and a desk. A room for patients to relax in, whatever their anxieties.

Ritva offered him coffee or a drink, both of which Arvo refused. He then went on to explain the purpose of his visit in more detail. In the course of his investigations into Mr Arvika's tragic death, he needed to build up some kind of picture of those associates who were nearest to him at the time in question. She would be aware that none of the actual performers were available now in the town but she and her husband were reported to have been reasonably familiar with at least a few of them and might be able to give some impressions of the kind of person each of them was and of the relationship between them.

Ritva paused slightly before responding.

'Perhaps you could be more explicit. What exactly do you want me to tell you?'

'How well did you know Mr Arvika himself?'

'I've been slightly acquainted with him for some years: this isn't the first time he's sung in the Festival. But only as an occasional guest accompanying his wife to our villa in Punkaharju and sometimes at receptions and on other social occasions connected with the Festival. His wife, Eeva, I know somewhat better.'

'Ah yes. Mrs Arvika. She seems to have shown remarkably little interest in the death of her husband. In fact, we haven't yet been able to locate her though she surely must have seen accounts of it in newspapers, and it seems rather curious that she made no inquiries about him on his disappearance. One can only assume they were separated.'

'I hardly think it can still be a secret that Eeva had left him, after years of loyal cooperation. I know nothing at all about the cause of their separation. Peik was indeed a difficult person in many ways: good-looking, charming, even fascinating when it suited him, an excellent singer, at least earlier in his career, but morally and emotionally an undeveloped child: spoilt, selfish and completely unreliable. He set out to attract women with considerable success and was perpetually unfaithful to Eeva. And for a long time he drank to excess, not, I should say, as an alcoholic, but as a means of asserting his virility, in fact of showing off.'

'What was his wife's attitude to all this?'

'She was typical of a certain kind of Finnish woman: old-fashioned perhaps nowadays but still in existence. I'd guess that she was infatuated with him when they married but almost certainly discovered her mistake only too soon after. But she felt she'd taken on a responsibility and would see it through. And he knew well enough how to play on her feelings: he would act the charming but naughty child, turning to mother for forgiveness and comfort.'

'So he never actually left her?'

'Indeed no. She was far too useful to him. As a mother-substitute and as a singer who was soon as famous as himself —he'd met her, I believe, when she'd been a student. In fact in the first place it had been he who'd created her. In time, however, their positions were reversed. His drinking and womanizing had made him a very unreliable performer both on stage and off. Concerts had to be cancelled and last-minute substitutes called in if any were available and his singing and personal appearance were deteriorating all the time until finally he was virtually unemployable. At this time Eeva became his main source of income.'

'How did he come to be singing in Savonlinna, then?'

'When the performers were first selected, he wasn't even considered. Then, I think it was in March or thereabouts, the first choice had to cancel his contract and his understudy, Mr Hannu Hietanen, took over the rôle. Eeva had already been accepted as Donna Anna and when rehearsals started, her husband was always in attendance. He'd apparently changed completely. He'd given up all forms of alcohol and, by all accounts, was behaving as a model husband. In fact he was said to be almost over-polite and helpful. Finally he begged the director to be considered as official understudy, taking responsibility for the expense of his costume himself. He'd had a lot of experience of the part and was now on occasion allowed to take over in rehearsals. Finally, from what I've heard, he was called upon to stand in when Mr Hietanen failed to appear for the opening of the final appearance.'

'Yes, I heard from the guide who took me round the Castle a rumour about Mr Hietanen's being assaulted and tied up in a barn on the night before that performance, and it would be interesting to learn more about that from Mr Hietanen himself. Would you know where he is now?'

'No, I'm afraid I don't. His home's in Helsinki and during rehearsals he returned there as often as he could so I didn't meet him socially. I'm sure the Festival direction could help you there.'

'I'd read somewhere that Mr Risto Aho, who was singing the part of Don Ottavio, is an old friend of Mr and Mrs Arvika, and has sung with one or the other in opera several times before.' Arvo paused.

'Are you asking some kind of question?' Ritva inquired.

Arvo wondered at the brusqueness of her tone: was something known to the doctor being concealed from him? He answered briefly, 'Only about the kind of person he was and maybe something of his relationship with the Arvikas.'

'He was a very old friend of Peik's, that I know, and in fact seems to have got on well with both of them. Some people find him lacking in personality, colourless perhaps, though he has an excellent voice. He tends to appear in less flamboyant parts like that of Don Ottavio.'

'Is he married?'

'Not that I know of.' Again that oddly abrupt answer. 'But as I say, he's not an outgoing character: rather difficult to talk to.'

'And the Commendatore, let's see, Mr Ilmari Karhu, who must have been one of the last to see him alive. Do you know him well?'

'Quite well.' Ritva spoke decisively. 'He's the kindest and sincerest person I've ever met, with a high intelligence and wide interests. But though he's a highly-trained singer, he devotes much of his life to the welfare of animals—and people. He still trains as a singer and continues to give concerts if he's sure of being free for them—he has a partner who shares his practice. Most of the time, however, he lives quietly in the country in a village near Lahti. I'd suggest your applying to him for information about the actual performance.'

A bell rang and she paused to listen to the maid on her way to the door. At the sound of the voice outside she turned to the detective.

'I'm sorry, that's my first patient and I have a long list of appointments. Is there anything else essential you'd like to know?'

'Perhaps you could give me Mr Karhu's address and telephone number,' Arvo requested.

She wrote quickly on a piece of paper detached from her appointments pad and handed it to him before rising and opening the door of her consulting room. Arvo thanked her and made his way to his coat and the outer door, thinking as he did so: She could have told me a lot more that now I suppose I'll have to find out from other sources.

2. COFFEE WITH THE COMMENDATORE

Ilmari had made his home in a typical straggling Finnish village some twenty miles from Lahti, a town of somewhat impersonal apartment blocks, the fourth largest in Finland. The surrounding countryside was undulating and forest-covered, the now yellowing foliage of birches and the sombre green conifers beneath an overcast sky reflecting yellow, green and heavy grey in the many lakes in the neighbour-hood.

An appointment had been made over the telephone and Ilmari appeared at the door as Arvo's car drew up outside the gate. He opened the gate and led Arvo through his small front garden, bright with chrysanthemums and dahlias, and into a wooden house, deep red in colour, awaiting it seemed its natural frame of contrasting snow over garden, trees and bushes and covering the roof from which long glittering icicles would gradually prolong themselves towards the snow blanket below.

The sitting-room was furnished simply in country style with plain but well-made table, chairs and cupboards, the handiwork of local craftsmen, and only the desk and book-case of modern teak. A large ceramic stove which had once been used for sleeping on during cold winter nights occupied one corner. A coffee-kettle protected by a cosy was ready on the table, together with slices of pulla, and as soon as his coat had been deposited in a small outer hall, Arvo was invited to sit down.

'Have you come from Savonlinna,' he was asked, 'or is this a matter for the Helsinki police department?'

Ilmari was pouring coffee as he spoke and as Arvo watched him he realized he had seldom seen such a serene face though an over-serious one, despite the smile-lines engraved on it. There was no doubt of some recent Russian ancestry. In photographs of the cast he had studied in Savonlinna he had noted the narrow deep-blue eyes and Slav, even Tartar, facial structure. He had heard too that this Commendatore spoke Russian and was in the habit of visiting that country. Could there conceivably be some kind of Russian or political involvement here? It was a fleeting thought, quickly dismissed. He turned his attention to Ilmari's question.

'A case of this kind must inevitably be dealt with at national level. Apart from other considerations, the people involved are all so scattered by now: some of them almost certainly abroad. I anticipate having to travel considerably in my investigations.'

A late wasp was showing interest in the bread and sugar. Ilmari opened a window and, trapping it gently in a small tablemat, shook it out where it darted off across the garden. He returned to his place at the table.

'That must indeed cause a lot of difficulties,' he observed. 'I suppose in most of your cases people all stay put more or less within a stone's throw of one another. And now the mountain has to go to many Mahomets.'

'What makes it even more difficult is that the mountain doesn't even know yet where half the Mahomets are. I suppose you can't help me with that aspect of the case?'

'I'm sorry, I can't. Only the Turunens, and Ritva Turunen has telephoned to say you've visited her already. I live very quietly here. And until last week I haven't been here even: this cottage was badly damaged in the Midsummer Eve storm and we've only just finished putting it to rights again for me to move back. I heard the news on the radio a day or two ago—of the finding of the body, I mean—so I rather expected some investigations to be made, especially in the case of those who'd possibly seen him last.'

'I believe you were one of them.'

'You know the opera I expect?' Arvo nodded. 'So you'll know that as Commendatore I had the job of carrying him off to hell. Actually down a short passage that comes out at the Suvorov Courtyard. Peik looked really ill then but he just told me he needed a moment alone: he'd be back in time for the curtain call. He then went ahead into the Courtyard. I waited for a few minutes in the passage and then realized I'd only just about time to make it myself. I had a quick look into the Courtyard but he was nowhere to be seen so I took it for granted he'd gone back some other way. The chorus members, that's to say the four devils who'd assisted me to drag him off, had gone straight off to the assembly point so there was nothing I could do but go there myself. There we all realized he wasn't with us, so some of us carried out a quick search: I checked the Courtyard again myself, but he couldn't be found. Dr Pavlov made an announcement from the stage that he'd collapsed as he could hardly admit that the principal singer was lost. We made a much more thorough search afterwards, at least a few of us did. Several of the others had to travel long distances that night so they were busy getting ready to leave.'

'But surely somebody would have been going home with Mr Arvika after the performance? His wife, for instance?'

'I understand that Mrs Arvika, Eeva, left with the Laufachs for Koli. I'm afraid that for various reasons, Peik wasn't too popular with anyone that evening.'

'Do you know why?'

'During the Second Act his performance deteriorated noticeably and it was assumed he'd been overdrinking. In fact it was my opinion he was ill, but most people thought otherwise and naturally it had made a bad impression on the audience.'

'And do you know why his wife should have decided to leave him—as apparently she did—just that evening?'

'The story going round was that he'd struck her. But it would surely be better to ask her about that.'

Again the shut door, the evasion, the sense that much was known but little was to be told. The Turunens, among the audience, had missed a lot of what was going on, but Dr Ritva had almost certainly known a good deal more than she'd admitted. Was this a concerted arrangement to shield somebody, some possible murderer? Or was it an attempt of a community to hush up scandals within its ranks? Arvo tried yet another tack.

'What were relations like between Mr Arvika and the director, Dr Pavlov?'

Ilmari answered without hesitation. 'They had very little to do with each other. Peik's rejection had in the first place been the responsibility of a committee, long before Dr Pavlov came into the picture. The first appointee for Giovanni was forced by circumstances to withdraw and the understudy, Hannu Hietanen, took over. Full rehearsals started early in June—I wasn't attending regularly then as I'd got only a small part—but Peik was present at all rehearsals. It's true, he had some sort of right to be there as his wife was singing the part of Donna Anna. He'd pulled himself together considerably and showed himself so interested that almost without anyone being aware of it, he became an unofficial understudy. And naturally he was specially polite and co-operative to Dr Pavlov.'

'And how did he come to be taking the main rôle on the evening in question?'

'Hannu Hietanen arrived half an hour late, so Peik had been asked to take over the part. Hannu's story was that he'd been knocked out the night before, tied up and left in a barn. He wanted to resume his rôle after the interval but Dr Pavlov managed to dissuade him. It wouldn't have been practical.'

An odd word, 'practical', Arvo thought. It could be interpreted in various ways.

'So Peik had taken over his part. Did Hietanen suspect that Peik might himself have been in any way involved in the matter?'

Ilmari was concentrating on pouring a second cup of coffee for Arvo and himself. He offered a plate of biscuits to his guest before replying, wondering just how much the Superintendent already knew.

'He mentioned a red Mercedes half-hidden near where he was attacked,' he said slowly. 'He had the impression it was similar to the one Peik drives.'

'Did he say anything about it to Peik?'

'He spoke about it to Dr Pavlov and me but I don't remember if Peik was present then. And as he said, he had no concrete evidence.'

'But he was angry with Peik?'

'For what he suspected, not what he knew. He's a reasonable sort of chap who wouldn't bear grudges without justification. And he accepted the fact that the replacement of a substitute half way through would have been awkward.'

'Did he leave the theatre at once?'

'I brought him something to eat as he hadn't eaten all day and I didn't see him again after that. I recall now that Eeva came into the room while Hannu was describing what had happened and she might have known something that would have confirmed his suspicions though she didn't say anything. Maybe Peik had been off somewhere in his car without giving any explanation. I think that might have been the moment she decided to leave him, but of course that's only speculation.'

Half-truths, embroidery, suppressions: without any knowledge of what Arvo had learned or would learn elsewhere, Ilmari was doing his best to divert suspicion from where it was not due. Arvo suspected this: it nearly always happened in an investigation, but he respected Ilmari none the less for it. He leaned back in his chair and looked across the table directly at his host.

'Have you any idea, even the faintest one, who might have committed this murder?' he asked, speaking as to a colleague or friend and not as a policeman. 'Somebody did. Somebody presumably who had a motive: revenge, fear, hatred, gain, necessity: I doubt whether greed or jealousy come into it, though who knows?'

Ilmari answered as a colleague or friend would have done. 'I'm no psychologist but I imagine that motives can be curious things. You could imagine that several people there might have had motives of a kind. Take any group of people and you might discover reasons for each of them to find the existence of one of the group inconvenient. But to put these reasons, these feelings, into effect, to terminate that existence in cold blood, would surely require a motive far stronger than the obvious ones you've mentioned. At least in the normal person, and there was nothing abnormal about the people present that evening.'

Arvo thanked his host for the coffee and rose to stroll across to the bookcase crammed with paperbacks in Finnish, Russian and English on a range of subjects that included travel, literature and music, besides the expected ones on wild life and the countryside.

'I'll be going to Sweden tomorrow,' he said. 'I'd like to have a chat with the Pavlovs. And while I'm there I'll probably drop in on a former summer-school English teacher of mine. She's teaching somewhere near Orrefors at present. She seems to like Scandinavia: until June of this year she was working in Savonlinna and might have known some of the people involved.'

Ilmari, who had been watching a silver tabby cat playing on the grass outside, swung round to face him. 'Not Miss Iris Lawton?' he burst out. 'You know her?'

'I do indeed. I was in her class in Canterbury two summers ago and since then we've kept in touch. She has visited my family twice and has now written to me about her new job. So you met her in Savonlinna? You wouldn't be that very pleasant vet who was also a singer she mentioned? Of course, you must be.'

'So you knew Iris had been in Savonlinna,' Ilmari said slowly.

'I see what you mean. Yes, I knew all right. There was another Miss Lawton with a different first name who somehow got mixed up with the Russians, wasn't there? A strange coincidence, yes: she must have been about Iris's age, I'd say. Not unlike her in a photograph I saw, either. Ah, but it was this Miss Lawton's first visit to Finland, wasn't it, so there couldn't have been any connection, could there?'

Ilmari grinned, the smile lines momentarily restored. He crossed to the desk where he obviously normally worked, opened the top drawer and drew out a framed photograph which seemed to have been hastily thrown inside, handing it to Arvo before replacing it in what was without doubt its normal position in front of a Finnish Grammar book in the centre of the desk. It showed an Iris retreating with a blend of horror and laughter on her face from a large frog which Ilmari, seen side-face, was extending towards her.

Arvo shared the grin. 'Yes,' he commented, 'that's Iris, our Iris. Not my business of course, but in the letter she sent us, she was wondering why she hadn't heard from you for quite a long time.'

He shook hands without further comment, put on his coat and strode through the door and along the garden path where a chill autumn wind was already detaching the bright yellow leaves and carrying them away into the distance as the first raindrops started to fall. Ilmari watched him get into his car, and turned away, his face now bleak and expressionless, as he mechanically removed coffee-cups and pulla from the abandoned table.

3. SWEDISH SANCTUARY

On returning to headquarters, Arvo applied for permission to carry his investigation to Stockholm, that elegant northern capital, which displays its Royal Palace, its Parliament buildings and its Town Hall alongside the broad river highway to the sea. Ostensibly he wanted to meet that larger-than-life character who could perhaps tell him more than anyone else, the director of *Don Giovanni*, who, according to Press reports, had found it necessary to abandon his own country to live in the West where he had been joined by his wife in circumstances that still remained obscure.

Permission having been given, he telephoned the Swedish police for cooperation and after some argument they supplied Andrei's unlisted telephone number. It was not until late in the evening that he could get an answer and was able by means of infinite tact, charm and reasonableness to make an appointment to see the director, though only at nine o'clock in the morning before he left for the theatre. Arvo set his alarm for four o'clock, crept out of the house without disturbing his sleeping family and took a taxi to Helsinki Airport, where he boarded a plane to Stockholm.

He reached the air terminal in the city shortly before eight o'clock when the ruthless and ferocious morning rush hour was at its height. With half an hour free before he must make his way to the appointment, he escaped the roar and screech of battle to wander peacefully through the narrow streets of the Old Town which had managed to preserve the homeliness and repose of times long past despite new paint, spotless window-glazing and shops displaying the latest experiments in glass and ceramics.

A taxi took him to the Pavlovs' rented apartment high on the fourteenth floor of a soaring new building overlooking the river. It was an unwelcoming Natasha who opened the door when he rang and who addressed him in cold precise English: 'Mr Laurila? My husband is expecting you.'

She led him into a sitting-room that was flooded with light and sunshine from the huge window overlooking the river. Andrei put down the copy of *Pravda* he had been reading and rose to shake hands.

'Don't be surprised at my reading-matter,' he said, in a powerful strongly-accented voice. 'Do you know, in this beautiful country, I find that publication really quite entertaining though I must say I rarely did in the country of its origin.'

Natasha hovering in the background, shook her head disapprovingly before suggesting the inevitable coffee or maybe Russian tea. Arvo decided on the latter and she went off to the kitchen.

'Poor Natasha,' Andrei commented, when they had both established themselves on only reasonably comfortable chairs of contemporary design, 'She really isn't happy here. The West seems to be living up to her worst expectations: violence, shameless women, luxury, waste. She's got no interest in the beauty of the city: she's aware only of the hopelessness of families looking for somewhere to live, extortionate rents, unemployment. She talks of the right of everyone to work and ignores the unemployment benefits, the pensions and all the other State care. She'll probably soon find evidence of exploitation and oppression too: you can always find it if you look hard enough.'

'Does she want to go back?'

'She's a Russian: of course she does. So do I. But not in my case to the present set-up. She's always been a good obedient Communist: it suits her temperament. It certainly doesn't suit mine. For me, to have to go back would be a nightmare. I'd do anything to avoid it. It's wonderful to have her with me: I would have been unbearably lonely without her. But I know she won't change. There are going to be problems for both of us and especially for her and I don't see any solution to them. But what is life without problems? I've got so much to be thankful for.'

Arvo wondered at the frankness of this man, after his earlier reluctance to meet him at all, and on a first encounter not with an individual but with a policeman who had come to interrogate him. The actual reason, the surge of relief Andrei was experiencing on meeting this pleasant-faced, relaxed, human representative of the law in place of the abrupt bullying State official, did not occur to him. Natasha's return, with a tray bearing small honey cakes and glasses in filigree metal holders containing golden-brown lemon tea, further dissipated any tension there might have been. She deposited cakes and tea on small tables and, with a suggestion of clearing up the kitchen, she retreated in that direction. Andrei called her back.

'You'll sit by me and help me with my English,' he said. 'And don't lecture me on the rights and place in the home of the Soviet wife,' he added.

'The place of the Soviet wife is at her husband's side,' Natasha responded, with a quick, teasing smile.

'Well, well, they actually taught you something back there that makes sense. These cakes are even better than usual, my dear.'

'May I have the recipe to take back to my wife,' Arvo asked, 'or is that classified as highly secret material not to be passed on to the enemy?'

'Of course you can, Mr Laurila. Have you any children?'

'Two boys of seven and nine.'

'They'll want a lot of them. Wait, I have many in the kitchen. I will get a bag.'

Arvo reflected on the transformation of the disapproving dogmatist into the warm-hearted and sympathetic homekeeper. Maybe temperaments could be changed and problems sorted out. He started to stuff the large package she gave him into his briefcase but with an 'Oh no, they will break in pieces,' she again rushed to the kitchen and brought back a plastic shopping-bag. 'You must carry that,' she said. 'It does not matter what people think.'

Andrei, who had brought out and lit his pipe, broke in now. 'We must remember my rehearsal,' he said. 'I will do my best to answer your questions, Mr Laurila, but I don't think I can help you much. What other people have you seen already?'

So here again is someone with something to hide, Arvo thought. He'll be calculating how much he can keep quiet and maybe lie about.

'I've visited the Turunens and Mr Karhu,' he replied aloud.

'The Turunens were in the audience so can tell you little. Mr Karhu was probably the last person to have seen Mr Arvika before the murderer.'

'So you don't think he could have been the murderer, himself.'

'Ilmari?' Andrei exclaimed. 'That would have been impossible even if he had had a motive. He had none; of that there can be no doubt.'

'So he was no enemy of Mr Arvika? He does seem to have been an exception.'

'He never judges people. He takes them as they come, not even excusing them, rather accepting them as they are and meeting them as friends.'

'How did you hear about the discovery of Mr Arvika's body?'

'Not in my *Pravda*, no. It was actually referred to on the BBC World Service, which I have listened to for many years. I then asked my colleagues for further information from the Swedish press.'

'So you will understand we have almost no on-the-spot indication of the identity of the murderer: no footprints, fingerprints and the like. We can't tell even exactly how he was killed except that he was dead when he entered the water and therefore likely to have been murdered. The exact time of his death is impossible to determine and people's memories of the sequence of events that evening will by now be confused. Mr Karhu has given his account of what happened at the end of the performance but we'd welcome yours as a check on his memory.'

Andrei's account of the exit from the stage and the disappearance of the principal singer coincided with that of Ilmari and he also referred to Ilmari's account of Peik's promise to be there for the curtain call. He himself had joined the others straight from the office, having left as soon as he'd heard the warning knock at the office door. He'd arrived just before Ilmari.

'What I find difficult to understand,' Arvo suggested, 'is why everybody seems to have taken Mr Arvika's disappearance for granted.'

'We searched for him twice,' Andrei explained. 'The second search was quite thorough and there seemed nothing more we could do. Hardly a matter for informing the police. Nobody was on good terms with him and he might have slipped back to his dressing-room while the announcement was being made, seized his clothes and taken them away somewhere to change so that he wouldn't have to face the others. It was dark enough by then for him to have got across the bridges without anyone paying much attention to him. How about his car?'

A point Arvo had neglected to investigate. Some time he must ask the Savonlinna police about it. Perhaps it was still parked somewhere near, or even had been stolen or 'borrowed' by local youths. He merely said, 'It hasn't been reported as found. And I've been wondering about Arvika's everyday clothes: burnt or buried or hidden somewhere. Plenty of places in the castle. Somebody must know. From what you say, any one of the people back-stage, including stage-hands, café staff and even visitors behind scenes, could have had the opportunity of committing the murder.'

'Technically speaking, yes, especially as no definite time can be established. But a motive could be found only among his professional associates.'

'By whom you must mean above all the other singers. Which of these can we probably eliminate?'

'All of them, I'd say. I can't imagine how the Masetto and Zerlina of the production, or for that matter Kaarina Laufach, our Elvira, or Eero Virèn who sang the part of Leporello, could possibly be involved. I don't think he had any connections with members of the chorus, including our four friends the devils, and we've already excluded Karhu.'

'Which leaves us with his wife and Hannu Hietanen, who indeed, from what I've already heard, had a rather strong motive if he was the type to bear grudges, and certainly he owed his escape only to a very lucky chance. Can you suggest anyone else?'

'Myself, naturally, I can't really think of a motive, though his singing was atrocious in the second act. And a very faint possibility, the quiet fellow Risto Aho, who was obviously very much attracted to Eeva Arvika. But he'd more or less followed her round for years without much hope and he'd as many qualifications for a murderer as the Ottavio character he was singing. After all, why should he, when it was clear that Eeva was walking out on her husband? And why in that event, should Eeva herself have taken the trouble to get rid of Arvika by violent means?'

'There remain two matters I would like to discuss with you,' Arvo mentioned. 'First, why after enduring him for years should Mrs Arvika have decided to leave her husband just that evening? Rather a strange coincidence, surely.'

'I understand they'd quarrelled about something.'

'You've no idea about what?'

'She may have heard something about the possible involvement of her husband in the removal from the scene of Hannu Hietanen.'

'What time did Hietanen actually arrive at the theatre?'

'I didn't notice. A half hour or so after the performance started, I think.'

'So you saw him?'

'Naturally. He came straight to me.'

'Intending to take over his part?'

'Yes.'

'Did he discuss the matter with anyone on the way?'

'I don't think so.'

'Where were you at the time?'

'In the office backstage.'

'Alone?'

'When he arrived, yes.'

'And later?'

'He was in a rather bad state physically so I called Karhu in.'

'And he came at once?'

'Almost.'

'So he witnessed what followed.'

Arvo paused before continuing, 'Hietanen was quite upset, I suppose, and demanded to take over his own part as soon as possible?'

'Yes, but I made it clear that that could not happen. It would have created a very unfortunate impression on the audience.'

'And he agreed?'

'Unwillingly, yes.'

'Did he leave then?'

'He thought it best not to in case he was seen, as this might lead to awkward questions. He was taken to an empty room and provided with refreshments.'

'When did he actually leave?'

'I've no idea.'

'So here is at least one person with both motive and opportunity.'

'Possibly. On the other hand, he wasn't the type to feel

such strong resentment and he'd have had nothing to gain by killing Arvika.'

'Was anyone else besides Karhu present in the office while this was happening?'

'Yes. Peik Arvika came in himself for a short time.'

'So he would have heard at least some of Hietanen's story.'

'Perhaps. So much has happened since then that I have no clear recollection.'

'But surely he'd have known about Hietanen's intention of taking over his part?'

'He must have done, I suppose.'

'And what was his attitude?'

'Naturally he'd have been very unwilling. But as I've said already, the idea would have been impractical anyhow.'

'I've got the impression that there were other people present. Eeva Arvika, for example?' The random arrow met its desired target.

'She came in for a few minutes after her husband.'

'Could she have heard anything then about her husband's alleged attempt to get Hietanen out of the way? Was that the reason for their quarrel?'

'I suppose it might have been. Believe me, Superintendent in all the confusion and excitement, with performers coming and going in the brief intervals they were off-stage, and after such a long interval, I have difficulty in recalling who might have been present or absent and what different people might or might not have overheard.'

'So there were additional people present at this time?'

'Only, I believe, Mr Aho, whom we've discussed already.'

Andrei, puffing vigorously at his pipe, was looking increasingly restless and uneasy while Natasha sitting at his side resembled more and more an enraged tigress ready to defend her mate. Arvo got up from his chair and wandered over to the window, watching the traffic moving noiselessly in the street below. He himself had lost something of his

relaxed friendliness as he turned again to confront the
director.

'What I find difficult to understand,' Arvo began, 'is why
exactly Hietanen, with almost certain suspicion that he'd
been cheated of his part by criminal means, meekly agreed
to resign it to the usurper. Opera audiences have sustained
greater shocks than being informed that the singer they'd
paid to see had now arrived, having been detained by an
accident, and would resume his rôle in the Second Act.
Unless,' Arvo paused, 'Mr Arvika had some more powerful
lever available. Are you sure, Dr Pavlov, that he had no
knowledge of your wife's presence in Finland—she'd still
have been in Finland at that time, wouldn't she. I wonder
if they'd warned you in your own country of the risk of
deportation from Finland of illegal immigrants.'

There was no immediate reaction, a rigidity, whether of
surprise or self-control delaying a response of any kind.
Finally Andrei said, 'Peik Arvika could have known nothing
of my wife's whereabouts or even that she had left the
Soviet Union. He would equally have known nothing of my
intention to come to Sweden. Only very few people had such
information and none of them would have been likely to
have confided in Peik Arvika of all people.'

Arvo came towards the couple with his hand outstretched.
'Well,' he said cordially, 'I won't keep you any longer: you
have other things to attend to.' He shook hands with his
host and hostess. 'Thank you again for the cakes, Mrs
Pavlov. My boys will appreciate them very much, I'm sure,
and my wife too. And now,' he added, as he made his way
towards the door, 'I plan to visit an old friend. An English
lady who spent several months in Savonlinna recently. You
may have met her. A Miss Iris Lawton. My former English
teacher. Goodbye for the present. And again thank you for
all your help.'

The silence that followed that piece of information re-
sounded deafeningly in his ears.

4. TESTIMONY OF AN ABSENT WITNESS

Arvo had telephoned Iris the previous evening at a number she had sent him on the back of a postcard showing the swelling form of a vase emerging in the moment of its creation by a glass-blower. He had explained that he would be coming to Stockholm to interview an important witness in a case he was investigating. At the same time there was a problem of no direct concern to her but on which he would welcome her advice.

Iris accepted the explanation without comment, merely informing him about a mid-morning plane from Stockholm to Kalmar which he might find useful if he was able to get to the airport in time for it. He could get a taxi from Kalmar to the glassworks and she'd be delighted to offer him lunch in the works canteen, assuring him that the food there would be infinitely better than her own hit-and-miss cooking.

Having left the Pavlovs soon after half past nine, he walked the short distance to the air terminal. It was a sunny morning with an invigorating chill to the breeze and there was an autumnal clarity of air, water and sky that made the mere fact of existence a delight. The bus from the terminal reached the airport a half-hour before take-off: a seat was available and soon he was moving serenely above a smooth fabric patterned in shades of green, gold and occasional blue: pines, firs and meadow grass, tawny garnered fields and orange speckles of autumn in massed birches, and lakes sprawled in their natural surroundings. A taxi carried him along the forty-odd kilometres separating Kalmar and Orrefors, winding through field, forest and villages of children's cut-out wooden houses, painted in ochre-red or the colour of cream itself.

On arrival at the white-tiled two-storeyed office block of

the glassworks with a prim garden before it, he was directed towards the canteen and found Iris adorning a seat nearby, intent on a very early page of a Swedish Grammar. She greeted him cheerfully and led him into a dining-room that was spotless and festooned with plants carefully disciplined to follow approved paths across window glass and surgically-white walls, or, in their potted variety, marking the exact centre of Formica-topped tables, each table with its complement of four matching chairs. The food was obviously rich in every worthwhile vitamin, the choice was wide, with emphasis on salad vegetables and sour milk products, and prices were low. Most of the works staff seemed already to have eaten and departed and Iris and Arvo carried their trays to a window table which provided a view of a car park with every available position occupied by an immaculate, carefully-positioned car.

After an exchange of news about family in Helsinki (or, as seen from the present location, Helsingfors) and the nature of the new job, Iris ended a pause by observing:

'And now Auntie Iris is ready with her motherly advice. What's the problem?'

'This morning I've been calling on an old acquaintance of yours together with his wife, with whom you had a much shorter acquaintance, at least according to the accounts I've read.'

Her eyes widened. 'You don't mean the Pavlovs?' she said. 'In Stockholm? Surely that hasn't got to be raked over again, has it? Are they—' the pronoun had a meaningful emphasis—'still insisting on inquiries?'

'They—' an echo of Iris—'do not address their inquiries to the criminal police. I assure you that what travellers (including our own and also British citizens) get up to within other people's boundaries, has no interest for us, unless of course it's a related to a crime in Finland itself. What does interest us is murder within our boundaries, as in the present instance.'

'Murder? Whose murder? If it happened in Finland, what's it got to do with Sweden?'

'Not a lot. But people do move about, you know, especially perhaps those who might know more than they should about a murder. Surely you know what murder I'm talking about?'

'Why should I? I hope it doesn't concern me in any way, though I hardly think it's likely. And just at present I'm living an ideal life without any access to news. Think how restful that is. I can't read the Swedish papers. Do tell me more.'

'Well, you should be interested. After all, it happened in Savonlinna.'

'In Savonlinna! That makes it real somehow, doesn't it. Nobody I knew there, I hope.'

'An acquaintance of yours at least, though I'd guess not a particularly close one. You might even consider he deserved to be murdered.'

'There's only one person who'd come into that category —Peik Arvika. But it's never the truly deserving who get their just deserts.'

'So he wasn't—what's the English expression?—your favourite pin-up boy.'

'And I'd hardly have been his favourite pin-up girl. But if it's really true, the murderer was surely an enraged husband.'

'Well, well, we hadn't considered that. That widens the field very considerably, I suppose.'

'If half the gossip of my Savonlinna housewives was to be believed, it would take in most of the husbands in Finland. A slight exaggeration perhaps, and anyhow it would date back a bit, with the husbands living elsewhere. The ladies were all waiting with bated breath to have the stories confirmed in Savonlinna but Peik had very obviously turned over a new leaf: in fact they were rather disappointed.'

'I'm not too happy about the enraged husband,' Arvo meditated, 'because from the inconclusive evidence we have, he was murdered at the end of the final performance of *Don Giovanni*. I doubt whether an outsider would have chosen that particular time.'

'How was he murdered?'

'He was washed ashore only a few days ago, carried by the currents from the direction of the castle, having been detained, we might say, in the Suvorov Channel. Do you know it?'

'I worked for a time as an English-speaking guide so I should. But how are you able to link it with the end of the final performance?'

'Among other things, because that was when he disappeared.'

Iris pushed away the tray she had been eating from, dislodging the pot plant two inches from its appointed position. Impatiently she confronted her former pupil as if he were being a disruptive element in the English class. 'Arvo Laurila,' she exclaimed, 'you're either inventing all this as you go along or you're following through a cunning scheme to make me reveal that I know everything and was really the murderer myself. Presumably I was one of his uncountable jilted girlfriends but in this case he'd really met his match: I came back that evening from . . . wherever I was that evening, bashed him on the head and dumped him in the cold, cold water. I confess all: fortified with all those good Swedish vitamins, you will arrest me and take me back —I nearly said home—to Finland. Admit you're pulling my leg or tell me the whole story in chronological order.'

Watching a solitary Volvo backing out neatly—surely not someone playing truant?—Arvo started on an account of the evening's events. This included the legitimate Don Giovanni's late arrival, the substitution by Peik, Hannu Hietanen's appearance, explanation and later withdrawal from his own rôle, Eeva's not yet fully understood decision to leave her husband forthwith and Ilmari's account of his last meeting with Peik. The story ended with the two vain

searches and the conclusion that Peik had gone off somewhere, not having the nerve to appear in public. He waited
for Iris's comment.

'So you've really got no idea who could have been responsible?'

'I think it's narrowed down to two, possibly three or four
possibilities. Hietanen, who'd had his rôle taken from him
after being mugged or drugged or both, and then tied up fo
hours—hardly the treatment which would endear his rival
to him, though we're not absolutely sure yet that Arvika
was responsible. Then there's Eeva Arvika who seems to
have been so upset that evening that it proved to be some
kind of last straw: her sudden decision to leave him after
years of endurance makes that clear. What makes things
really difficult is that everyone I've questioned is clearly
hiding all sorts of things, probably from motives of loyalty,
though who knows?'

'Which people have you seen already?'

'Not many yet. The Turunens first, though I can't imagine they're implicated, as they left half way through the
performance, unless one of them slipped back for some
reason.'

'The Turunens had other fish to fry that evening,' Iris
volunteered, 'though don't ask me what fish.'

'I see,' said Arvo thoughtfully, as if filling in an interesting
but not specially relevant gap in his knowledge. 'And then
there was your boyfriend, Ilmari Karhu.'

'My boyfriend no longer, not that he ever was,' Iris said,
with some asperity. 'I haven't heard a word from him since
I left Finland.'

'Has he got your address?'

'He could easily have found it out from the Turunens if
he'd wanted to.'

'Give the poor fellow a chance. He's only just moved back
into his house, which was pretty badly damaged in the
Midsummer storm.'

'Anyhow it doesn't much matter. Did you find out anything from him?'

'Some facts. Quite a lot of evasions.'

'Do you think he knows who the murderer is?'

'If he does, he's being very careful to shield him—or her. And then I saw the Pavlovs this morning and they seemed just a bit upset. Tell me, what do you know of Risto Aho?'

Iris showed no great surprise at the sudden change of subject.

'Almost nothing,' she responded. 'Nobody knows anything about Risto Aho: he's extremely shy and withdrawn, though it may be that still waters run very deep. I suspect he's quite considerably in love with Eeva Arvika, has been for years, I was told. But certainly not the type to murder her husband. And if Eeva was leaving Peik anyway, he wouldn't have spoilt any future hopes he might have had by becoming a murderer.'

'Other circumstances we don't yet know about might have pushed him to extremes. To change the subject slightly, when did you last see Arvika?'

Iris's mind went back to a night of unforgettable beauty, drama and regret. 'Shortly before I returned to England,' she said slowly, recalling again the huge clouds rolling up from the west and the rain quenching relentlessly the exultant magic of flames in lake water. 'It was Midsummer Eve and a crowd of us were visiting the Laufachs in their Koli villa. Not that I saw much of Peik then: he was off jogging somewhere, unless he was really sitting in his car listening to an argument between Ilmari and me.'

'If I might be so indiscreet, what were you and Ilmari arguing about?'

'I'd kept quiet about my volunteering to carry out a certain job that he thought, quite rightly, I wasn't really capable of doing. And he'd just found out about it from others concerned. We were standing in a lay-by some way above the villa, which is on the lakeshore, and he really was annoyed. And then it started pouring with rain and we had to leave in a hurry.'

The picture forming itself in Arvo's mind was hardly a clear one though he was in no doubt about the nature of the 'certain job' Iris had volunteered for. However, there was only one essential fact he must probe for. 'Why did you think he might have been listening?' he asked.

Iris gave a brief accoint of Ilmari's discovery in the car park: the red Mercedes with a window that had probably been opened during their conversation and certainly closed after their departure, suggesting strongly that the car's occupant had been eavesdropping on what they had been saying.

'Let's use unequivocal language for once, Iris.' Detective-Superintendent Laurila was now interrogating his witness. 'Did you discuss the arrangement for getting Mrs Pavlov out of Russia? I've no intention of reporting your answer back to the Finnish Foreign Office, who wouldn't be much interested anyhow, so you can tell the truth.'

'That's surely obvious already.'

'And arrangements for her arrival?'

An uncomfortable idea was beginning to stir in Iris's mind, 'I think so,' she admitted reluctantly.

'So Peik Arvika, as it seems very likely that he was indeed listening, would have known that Natasha Pavlov would be in Finland on approximately a certain date and exactly where.'

'But there was the storm: the thunder was terrific and you can't be sure he heard anything properly.' What suspicions might be passing through the mind of her respectful pupil, now transformed into a Grand Inquisitor?

Her fears were by no means allayed by his reply. 'True,' he agreed, 'but what you've told me gives substance to an idea I've already considered about just why Hannu Hietanen was pressed into accepting so meekly the loss of his rightful part. And just what mischief Peik Arvika could have set afoot even after that if he hadn't been destroyed in time. Don't look so miserable, Iris: it would have come out sooner or later. What I'd like to do now is to see round these glassworks. You never had the chance of guiding me round Olavinlinna which I'd have very much enjoyed but I can still test your guiding qualifications here in Orrefors, can't I?'

5. FISHING AT THE SEASIDE

Feeling slightly uneasy about reactions from the accounts department to the inclusion of too many inland flight fares as expenses, Arvo took a train back to Stockholm, sleeping throughout the journey. He felt no such hesitation about flying back to Helsinki and was in his own home before ten. With an unspecified number of other interviews in store, he realized he would have to report to headquarters some time the following day, which was a Saturday, and normally available for taking his family to their island villa for the weekend.

Three items were awaiting his attention when he eventually arrived in his office: an internal memorandum and two letters, one of the latter in a pale-green envelope with the neatly-arranged address on it in a feminine hand, the other in a buff-coloured envelope marked *Helsingin Sanomat*—the name of a high-circulation newspaper—and with his own name typed on it.

He extracted the memorandum from its cover and studied the Finnish information shown, which amounted in English to the following details:

PRESENT LOCATIONS AND WORKPLACES OF:
1. Arvika, Eeva.
Liisantie 86B52

Helsinki.
Finnish National Opera, Helsinki.

2. Aho, Risto.
Hotelli Esplanaadi
Helsinki.
Finnish National Opera, Helsinki.

3. Hietanen, Hannu.
Raumankatu 25
Puistola, Kotka.
Kotka Theatre.

Arvo raised his eyebrows slightly at the third item. What on earth was Hietanen doing in Kotka, that small port some 180 kilometres east of Helsinki and no very great distance from the Russian border? He vaguely recalled having stayed there once with a great-aunt who had insisted on taking him to a performance of *The Merry Widow* at the local theatre, nothing of which he now remembered. He had not forgotten the harbour, however, where, as a young teenager, he had wandered along the quayside examining cargo boats from what then had seemed to him every port in the world. Could Hietanen be dignifying Viennese operetta in the unassuming little theatre in Keskuskatu—the Central Street of this remote, unromantic port, whose one memorable event had been its shelling by a British fleet, by all accounts on its way to the Crimean War via the Gulf of Finland.

The pale-green envelope aroused his curiosity, the more so as the flap showed no name and address of the sender. He slit open the top and on notepaper of a similar shade, read the following, written in English:

My dear Arvo,
    After so many years you will no longer remember your old schoolfriend Eeva Ruuskanen from Yhteiskoulu—the

mixed Grammar School in Turku. I seem to recall we were in fact secretly engaged for some three months and you helped me with my English translations much longer than that.

I'm afraid that my married name is probably much better known to you now. Dr Ritva Turunen has told me you are investigating my husband's death and I shall be very pleased to help you in every way I can.

I am spending the weekend with friends in Jyväskylä. One of them has a cabin cruiser and we plan to spend much of Sunday sailing down Päijänne to Heinola or even as far as Lahti.

How about joining us on our excursion? You are welcome to spend Saturday night on the boat though it might be a bit chilly and lonely there. Alternatively there is a very early plane from Helsinki and you could easily be here for nine o'clock when we plan to leave.

Incidentally, Risto Aho, who was one of the *Don Giovanni* cast, plans to join us, travelling from Helsinki overnight by train. You may well be able to learn something from him.

I'm sorry to have left this rather till the last minute but my telephone number is below. Please do let me know whether you can come. I promise nobody will worry you with questions, though you may ask us anything you like.

> Yours sincerely,
> Eeva Arvika.

Arvo replaced the letter slowly in the envelope, pondering. The invitation was in many ways opportune but would need consideration. He did indeed remember the lively schoolgirl and even their engagement, though he had quite forgotten how it had ended. From her publicity photographs Eeva appeared to have changed considerably, which was only to be expected. He would decide later what to do.

The last letter, no more than a note, was scribbled in English and ran:

Arvo,
    I've just picked up what may be an interesting piece of information for you. According to reports, you're working on the Savonlinna case, so I'm passing it on for what it's worth. I got it from one of the Press Attachés . . .

The telephone started ringing just as he reached these words. He raised the receiver absent-mindedly, snapping to attention as he heard the Chief Superintendent at the other end. The powerful voice sounded relaxed, however, and with good reason. Its owner had just dropped in to see if anything needed urgent attention before going off on a fishing trip and it had just crossed the CS's mind that Arvo might be in his room and if so to ask him whether he had unearthed anything useful during his Stockholm trip. As a fishing companion was waiting below in a car, he requested Arvo to call in at his office at once and summarize his findings.

Arvo folded and replaced the letter, stuffing it into his pocket automatically and went to report his interview with the Pavlovs. Nothing definite yet, was the Chief Superintendent's opinion, and he hoped there wouldn't be, though at present Dr Pavlov did seem the most likely candidate, a regrettable possibility involving extradition proceedings and other complications beyond anyone's imagination.

'Have you any plans for today?' he inquired next.

'I've just got the address of Hannu Hietanen, the fellow I mentioned in my earlier report, who should have been singing the main rôle but was abducted, probably by Arvika, who's said to have wanted the part for himself. He seems to have taken it all surprisingly mildly, much too mildly, I'd have thought, and so far it hasn't been discovered what he was doing for the rest of the evening after he turned up late.

That's why I'll phone to see if he's there and if he is, go and find out.'

'Do you know where he lives?'

'Kotka, according to the memo I received.' He brought out his notebook with the memo in it and read out Hannu's address.

'I started my police career in Kotka,' the Chief Superintendent mused. 'Arresting drunken seamen in ten different languages, with action not speech in the case of the other twenty languages in which I couldn't say "You're under arrest". Let's see: Puistola: a quiet suburb near the sea, but everything in Kotka's near the sea. Try the number and see if he's there.'

Arvo dialled the number and was answered by what sounded like an elderly woman. Hannu was brought to the phone and proved willing to give his version of the evening's events.

'I've been expecting something of the kind ever since I read about the discovery of the body. When would you be coming?'

Arvo looked at his watch. 'If I leave here at twelve, I should be in Kotka around two,' he reckoned. 'Would that time suit you or have you anything else fixed for the afternoon?'

'I'll be heating the sauna for later this afternoon, maybe about four, but you won't surely have all that much to ask,' Hannu said.

Arvo replaced the receiver and reported the arrangement to his superior, who expressed his approval and asked what other witnesses Arvo intended to see.

'It's the others who want to see me, it seems,' Arvo told him, 'or at least one of them does. An old girlfriend of mine, it turns out: Eeva Arvika. According to her, we were once engaged to be married.' Momentarily Arvo envisaged himself with a world-famous opera star cooking his dinner for him instead of his quite unglamorous but cheerful nursery-school-teacher wife. 'She's written to invite me on a cruise on a friend's yacht: to be more exact, a Sunday trip on a cabin cruiser leaving Jyväskylä tomorrow. Is it from her that I'll learn all, do you think? She doesn't seem to have remembered our brief romance till now.'

'Has she included your wife and family in the invitation?'

'Well, no. I doubt whether she's thought of them. Supposing I just turn up with them at my side?'

The Chief Superintendent laughed, wished him good hunting (or fishing maybe) and left the room to join his patient and accordingly well-qualified fisherman friend, while Arvo went off to pick up his briefcase from his office, thence to make his way to a small restaurant at the end of the street, where he worked his way through a lunch of meatballs and boiled potatoes washed down with a glass of milk and followed by a rice porridge sprinkled with cinnamon. He rang his wife to give her an estimate of the time he'd be back for his evening meal and to break the news of a Sunday also away from home, without thinking it essential to inform her he would be spending the day with a former fiancée, now suspect in a murder case. Policeman's wives have to learn to take things in their stride but even the most long-suffering might balk at a Saturday cancellation of an island weekend while her husband went jaunting to Kotka, followed by a Sunday living it up on a cabin cruiser with a former fiancée, now a world-famous opera singer.

He reached Kotka shortly before two along the fast highway that connects the town with Helsinki, drove over the bridge that links Kotka to the mainland, past a bus station and a football stadium abandoned for the winter, finally locating a rural-looking suburb of pleasant small houses each in its own garden. Thankfully, as he left his car, he noted that the plume of smoke from the paper works was bearing its perfume of hydrogen sulphate—its Kotka money-smell—in the opposite direction. As he approached

the neat house he had been directed to, the door opened
and an elderly bright-eyed woman ushered him into a
sitting-room crowded with tables, chairs, a rocking-chair, a
television, stereo equipment, photographs of weddings and
christenings going back some sixty years and plants ram-
bling off over windows, walls and even the ceiling. Coffee
was offered and politely refused and a stocky round-faced
man appeared from the cellar where he might well have
been doing things about the heating of the sauna. Muttering
'Hietanen' he shook hands and indicated a chair for Arvo
to sit on, its back to a wickerwork flower-pot holder and
with two huge Amaryllis lilies gazing down on the top of
Arvo's head. Clearly overawed by the presence of the police,
the woman withdrew. With little sign of sharing her respect,
Hannu took the offensive.

'I was expecting something like this,' he challenged from
a hard tapestry-backed chair, moved to an angle which
avoided direct eye confrontation.

Arvo was considering the implications of the 'this' while
he replied, 'Naturally, in any case we have to see everybody
who might have been in the least concerned.'

'What other people have you seen already?'

Yet another indication of a likelihood of circumspect
evasion? Arvo side-stepped by combining truth with vagueness, 'Some five or six people.' To avoid inquiries about
exact identities, he continued without pause, 'I was told
about your willingness to surrender your part in the opera.
In the circumstances I suppose it was the only decent thing
to be done, though a more selfish and also a more vindictive
man might have found a way of justifying obstinacy, whatever the results. He could, for example, have refused to
believe that Peik Arvika would have carried out his threat
or would have suggested ways of removing the lady from
her hiding-place before she could be discovered.'

Arvo waited for the reply with considerable anxiety. Had
he made a complete fool of himself forcing pieces of the

jigsaw together because at just one point there seemed a connection? Hannu, however, was not creasing or raising his brows in mystification as he replied, 'I've got a great respect for Dr Pavlov and a greater contempt for Peik Arvika. He seemed almost off his head at times. He was obsessed with that part, in particular on that final evening, and he'd have committed murder for it: nearly did, in fact, the night before. You'll have heard about that already, of course. I've wondered since when he'd have come back to release me, if at all. At the time he was issuing his ultimatum I'd got no idea what everything was about, certainly not that Mrs Pavlov was actually in Finland or the trouble that might create. Besides, the part itself didn't seem all that important by then and I can't say I really felt up to it. Anyhow, from a purely selfish point of view, helping Pavlov could have had—can have, I hope—later advantages.'

'So it wasn't just the effect it might have had on the audience?'

'No. At that point Pavlov had made it quite clear I was to take over. It was Arvika's threat that changed things. And so when the situation was explained in full, I agreed.'

However confusing the account, Arvo had got the information he'd been angling for. He now had to straighten things up.

'What I'd like to get clear are your own experiences, in the order they occurred, if you can remember. What actually happened to you the night before, so far as you're aware, and how were you able to get to the theatre the following evening?'

Hannu smoothed his hair back over his scalp as if this reminder of the leaden head he had awakened with might help in recalling every detail of what had happened, and then launched into what appeared a comprehensive and reliable account. He concluded:

'I got to the theatre at around quarter to nine and went straight to the backstage office.'

'Who was in there?' Arvo's question followed briskly.

'Only Pavlov, and when he saw me he went for Karhu, who had the sense to provide me with some brandy which helped a lot.'

'And Arvika?'

'He came in just after for a grumble and when he saw me he went off the deep end. When Pavlov said I was to take over the part, he started making his threats.'

'What were his actual words?'

'I haven't the least idea now. Something about a lady entering the country illegally and being at the Turunens' house: it meant nothing to me.'

'That's good enough,' said Arvo with satisfaction. 'And you three were the only other people present?'

'Yes. No. I think Eeva Arvika came in just before. It was after he'd made the threats that she said she was going to leave him.'

'So it was blackmail that decided things. What was Arvika's reaction to what she said?'

'She started off by accusing him of blackmail but he didn't turn a hair: in fact he more or less ignored her. It was then that she said quite calmly she was leaving him.' Hannu gave a snort. 'Now I remember. She made it rather clear that it was her money he'd miss and he slapped her twice across the face and screamed at her. Then he rushed off, for his entry, I think.'

'And Eeva? What did she do then?'

'Nothing for the moment. All of us were flabbergasted, I guess: I wasn't looking at her in particular. It was then that I got round to asking what it was all about. Pavlov and Karhu talked it over in Russian for a bit and then Karhu put us on our honour, so to speak, to keep silent about it and told us about Mrs Pavlov getting out of Russia.'

'How many people were present then?'

'Pavlov, me, Karhu, and yes, Aho, Risto Aho. He'd come in a bit earlier.'

'Before or after the blackmailing?'

'There was a pause. 'I don't know. There was too much coming and going.'

'Before or after the assault on Eeva?'

'I remember now. He arrived just at the moment it happened. All he could do was to look as feeble as a sick sheep, as he usually does. Then Arvika pushed him out of the way to return to the stage for his entry.'

'Is there anything between Eeva Arvika and Aho?'

'He'd like there to be but I'd hardly think so. And I shouldn't pick him as the murderer, even though that reduces by one the number of those in the line-up.'

'Why not?'

'He'd never have had the nerve.'

'Who would have?'

'Come to think of it, all of us, at any rate while we were still in state of shock, even Risto Aho for a moment. Not Karhu that I remember, but then he was the bystander, nor the Doctor, Pavlov I mean, who restored order and brought us to our senses. But we're none of us maniacs and any murderer must be a bit off his head—or drunk—which none of us was.'

'So you agreed to stand down?' This was spoken as a question and Hannu nodded agreement. Arvo went on, 'What did you do after you'd decided?'

'If I'd gone home, as I wanted to, I might have been seen by somebody and that would have started speculation. So Ilmari Karhu took me upstairs to an unused room and brought me sandwiches, good chicken ones I remember, and beer. I locked myself in, drank the beer and then went to sleep. I'd had a trying day.'

'When did you wake up?'

'I think it was a ship's hooter that woke me. There's a tour that passes between the island and the town and one of the bridges has to be swung round to let it through. I'm not sure, though. I opened the door and could hear singing

below so the performance hadn't finished. But I still hadn't
wound my watch so I didn't know the time. Then about ten
or fifteen minutes later I could hear through the window
that people were crossing the bridge so I waited until things
were quiet again and then slipped out myself.'

'Did you meet any of the performers?'

'No. It was actually some time later and I imagine they'd
all gone.'

'What did you do after you'd left?'

'I returned to where I'd been staying, collected my things
together, got into my car and drove back to my family in
Helsinki. I gave my wife the shock of her life by arriving
around five in the morning but I'd had enough of Savonlinna. And to end the tale, here I am staying with my
grandmother rehearsing for the most ambitious undertaking
Kotka has had yet: *Tosca*. Would you believe it? Any more
questions? I want to see about that sauna.'

'Just two more things, if you don't mind,' Arvo suggested
in a conciliatory tone. 'First, how sure are you that it was
Arvika who attacked you?'

'Ninety-six per cent. There was the red Mercedes with
the Helsinki number. Then, whoever it was grabbed me
from behind. He was just that much taller than I was and
as he forced the cloth over my nose, I turned my head
towards his face trying to get away from it. And I remember
now feeling the short beard round his chin: Arvika had been
clipping his ready in case he'd need it like that. And think
of the circumstances: nothing was stolen and who else on
this earth would have wanted me out of the way just at that
moment?'

'Fair enough,' said Arvo. 'Then why didn't you go to the
police to bring charges against him? If only to justify yourself
in the eyes of the audience, your colleagues and the Press,
who might well have had something to say about your
apparent failure to turn up for the performance?'

'Oh, what would have been the point? The fellow had

disappeared, hadn't he? Actually some kind soul passed on
to the Press the tale that I'd been knocked down, which I
refused to confirm, and I got a lot of sympathy in the end.
Would you like to join me in the sauna?'

'No, I've got to get back, thank you all the same,' said
Arvo absently.

As he said goodbye to the grandmother, he was wondering
just how much of the evidence of this seemingly blunt and
frank young man was actually to be trusted, even though it
had indeed confirmed and supplemented a good deal of
what he had himself suspected.

6. THE LAST OF THE SUMMER WINE

'Everything in Kotka's near the sea,' the Chief Superintendent had said, and on leaving the Hietanens' house Arvo
decided to take a short break to revive old memories. So he
parked his car by the bus station and set off to circumnavi-
gate the island on foot. It was the kind of weather he
most enjoyed: a boisterous wind sending huge cream-cheese
clouds billowing across the sky, revealing and obscuring a
low autumn sun. He turned right in the direction of the oil
harbour, where a pungent aroma indicated the presence of
oil storage and the brief resting-place of tankers, but he did
not approach, merely turning south where he could look out
over green islands, the more distant of them outposts of the
Soviet Union. A turn to the left past the paper-factory and
he was pacing the remembered wharves, where even on
this Saturday afternoon ships were loading and discharging
(fewer now than he recalled) and a train screamed warning
of its approach. Back through the main street with its slightly
sordid-looking cafés to his car and a restful drive along
deserted roads to home and family.

During his walk and the return drive he had been juggling

with the assorted packets of information he had been given, trying inconclusively to classify them under motivation labels: gain, emotion (with the emphasis on hatred, jealousy, revenge, frustration, fear), together with political or maybe psychological considerations. There could of course be other factors that had escaped him: the facile threefold formula of gain, passion or fear being totally inadequate, as he well knew. He approached his home with a tinge of unease: his wife, he felt, had ample justification for greeting him with a blunt instrument in hand, but the combined family greeting reduced him to his proper humility. They were all three in the impassioned final stages of a game of Ludo and his wife's abstracted 'I suppose you want something to eat' would have been met with a 'No, I've just been having caviare and champagne with the Superintendent' if it hadn't reminded him he was starving.

Over a good homely risotto, he handed her the letter on green notepaper as a prelude to his justification of tomorrow's absence. Her comment was not unexpected.

'I see. It comes now to flaunting the other women in your life. Scented notepaper indeed. I thought you had better taste.'

'Is it?' he responded, sniffing it with slight aversion. 'But this one was before I met you. I've been educated since then.'

'An actress.' Her button nose twitched.

'A singer, not an actress.'

'An opera singer, so if she's not an actress she's no good. And the wife of a Don Giovanni.'

'More to be pitied than condemned, surely. How would you like to be the wife of a Don Giovanni?'

He had let himself in for it. 'Eeva and I obviously have things in common,' she retorted, her voice ice-cold. 'Why did she throw you over?'

'How do you know she did?' he asked, racking his brain for the long-forgotten reason. 'Anyhow she didn't. It was by common consent. We were both leaving school and our ways lay apart.'

'Did you give her a ring?'

'Possibly. But she wouldn't have worn it in public: it was a secret engagement.'

'It wasn't the one you gave me, by any chance?' she queried, with apparent misgiving.

'What curious minds women have!' he countered. 'As if it would have mattered. You should be pleased at my concern for economy. I remember now: we bought it together at Tempo.' Tempo had been the local dime-store. 'Is that where yours came from?'

She pondered a bit. 'Does she know you're married now?'

'How should I know? I doubt whether she's concerned.'

'No, she probably wouldn't be. Anyhow she's being very useful. Matti offered to take me and the children to his summer cottage tomorrow. His car's just about big enough for us three.'

'Oh, there'll be room enough for Annikki, I'm sure. I can't see her staying at home. I wish I were coming.'

She gave over teasing and grinned at him. 'So do we, love. Never mind. I didn't do so badly in the marriage stakes. I'm sorry for that Eeva Arvika. Someone should have knocked off that Peik years ago. On humanitarian grounds. I hope it doesn't rain.'

A six o'clock start the following morning got him to the airport with half an hour to spare, so he bought two newspapers, *Kansan Uutiset*, a far left journal, with glowing accounts of neighbouring Five-Year-Plan achievement statistics, and *Aamulehti*, a right-wing Tampere paper, wallowing in gloom about the current Finnish unemployment figures. Such was the nature of democracy. And yet it survived.

Jyväskylä, positioned more or less in the centre of sub-Lapland Finland, had always seemed to him a town without character, colourless, flavourless and chill. There was an

inconveniently-designed Aalto university complex sup-
plementing older, pleasanter and more practical buildings,
a narrow green 'ridge' through the centre of the city, along
which joggers jogged, the more sedate citizens exercised
their dogs of impeccable pedigree and the younger ones
their talents for less worthy activities. A bus took him from
airport to terminal and from there it was a short step to the
departure point at the lakeside.

He recognized the point in question as only one boat of
the prescribed class was still afloat. The boat appeared to
be unoccupied though one or two potential passengers were
waiting alongside. A couple were sitting on a seat nearby
gazing at it fixedly and a tall pleasant-looking man of his
own age moved restlessly to and fro, intent on any car that
approached, though in the first ten or so cases all failed to
stop. At a quarter to nine two men who might from their
attire have been the owners or at any rate the crew emerged
from a taxi, greeted the seated couple and all five embarked.
A second couple followed in another taxi, and went aboard
and there was the sound of excited greetings. Arvo and the
pacing man exchanged occasional questioning glances until
the latter froze in his tracks watching the approach of a blue
Volvo. When it drew up, a woman in a perfectly-tailored
olive-green trouser-suit emerged, turned to say a few last
words to the car's occupants and came towards them. She
kissed his companion lightly on one cheek and whispered a
few words while glancing quickly with a smile towards Arvo
and then came up to him, throwing her arms round him
and kissing him warmly on each cheek.

'How wonderful, Arvo! So many years and you haven't
changed in the very least, except, well, to expand a bit
maybe and get just a bit older.' She stepped back holding
him at arm's length and examined him. 'Oh, Arvo, you look
so distinguished now: a Siegfried I think or a Sarastro. How
stupid I was! I admit now: it was all my fault we quarrelled.'

The nature of the quarrel evaded him still but Arvo was

never one to be outdone. 'I'd never have recognized you. You were much the prettiest girl in the class but I'd have grovelled at your feet in apology if I'd had any idea you'd grow into a Miss Finland.'

She pushed him away and laughed, turning to Arvo's silent companion. 'Did you hear that, Risto? You men are all alike. Andrei telephoned yesterday to say he'd been visited by a police superintendent, one Arvo Laurila, investigating my husband's death. I said I'd been engaged to him years ago and he said he regretted to tell me that the superintendent who'd called now had a wife and two children. And he, a respectable married police-superintendent comes and flirts with me like this! Arvo this is Risto, a dear lifelong friend of myself and of my late husband. He'll be coming with us today.'

Risto bowed very slightly and shook hands formally, muttering his name in Finnish fashion. He followed silently as Eeva ushered Arvo on to the boat and stood in the background while general introductions were being made, taking his turn later to be presented to all and sundry as Risto Aho, 'an old friend of my late husband'. One of the unknown men was a lawyer with a dentist wife, while the other, an architect, had a dress-designer wife. They knew Eeva slightly but, as guests of the owner of the boat, showed little interest in their fellow passengers. Arvo observed them, as he was trained to observe everyone he met, but though he could have described their appearance in detail if required later, he retained little impression of their personalities.

Once the boat left, the passengers all made themselves at home in a saloon of near-luxury surrounded on three sides by panoramic windows. As Risto hesitated momentarily in finding a place to sit, Eeva laid her hand on his shoulder gently. 'Arvo and I have fifteen years to catch up on,' she said, 'and also a good deal to discuss that's far more recent: I'm sure you can guess what that is. As soon as we've got the whole matter settled and Arvo requests to be put ashore immediately to hunt down and arrest the murderer we've identified, I'll be seeking your opinion on our brilliant deductions.'

'If you think I'm the murderer, I hope you'll deliberately mislead him.' Risto was smiling gently. 'That would relieve me a lot, Eeva, since you could persuade anyone of anything.' He moved to a seat that was out of earshot but from which he could watch her every movement.

Having implied her willingness to reveal all, Eeva sat silent and withdrawn for a considerable time, gazing ahead at the paper-mill desecrating the lake shore. The engine came to life with a subdued roar and the prow of the boat moved forward and away from the shore to cut a gleaming arc through the dark water so that the sun skimmed rapidly from right to left across the bows and sank to touch the tree-furred ridge of the low hills rising from the far shore. The roar muted to a contented purr and the powerful craft sped through an unpeopled world of light and darkness, a milk-white sky above sombre conifers splashed with the sunlit gold of birches.

It was as they approached the narrowing outlet from the lake to the south that she spoke at last. 'It's the funeral tomorrow,' she said.

'I know. I read about it in *Aamulehti*. Will you be there?'

'No. His family are arranging it. And there'd be a scene, a horrible one, if I turned up. I can well imagine they think I murdered him.'

'What are they like?'

'Cold. Snobbish. Clannish. He was their adored child whom I managed to trick, seduce and do my best to destroy. Peik took me to meet them soon after our marriage and they made it quite clear then that that visit was to be the last. He sees—saw—them occasionally and didn't spare me what they said about me.'

'So he was on their side?'

'He wasn't on anybody's side. He was the only boy and nothing and nobody was good enough for him. And he despised them: called them narrow-minded puritanical stick-in-the-muds.'

'Did he identify you with anyone in particular?'

'Inevitably with his mother, who'd always comfort and spoil her precious little darling. When he knew I was furious with him, he'd become the naughty little boy wheedling mother into forgiving him: when he wanted money—and he often did in recent years—he'd coax and plead as if it were a toy or a special treat he wanted. And I'd give in, as probably his mother had: you can't be a real-life Don Giovanni without being an adept at all the arts of getting what you want. He could be irresistible when it suited him and completely callous when it didn't. And when he started drinking heavily, some three years after we'd married, and there were unending disputes, cancellations and awful performances so that eventually he was cold-shouldered everywhere, I became mother the provider.'

The boat veered slightly to give wide berth to a small cable-ferry with four cars aboard and the sun shone direct into Eeva's face, high-lighting small frustration lines over her brows and a drawn look to eyes which all her skill with make-up couldn't hide. She turned away impatiently from the sudden brilliance and Arvo sensed the control she was exerting over half-buried misery, reawakened by memory.

'And you didn't leave him?'

'For better, for worse: that's what I'd promised. And divorce seems the easy way out, a running-away from a common enough problem. If he'd been violent I'd have left him and let him divorce me if he'd wanted to. But you can't live eight years with someone without developing some ties.'

'But you did decide to leave him finally.'

'On the night he disappeared? Yes, you'll have heard about that. But you wouldn't know, because I was the only one who did, that there wasn't the least doubt that he'd

been the one who'd attacked Hannu Heitanen and tied him
up for a night and a day, even leaving him there to starve,
maybe, just to get his part.'

'How do you know?'

'There'd been a farewell get-together the evening before:
we were all hurrying off after the final performance. It
wasn't planned to be one of those all-night affairs and in
fact it was only eleven o'clock when Peik suggested leaving:
he said he felt very tired. But we'd been home only a short
time when he started pacing up and down saying he needed
fresh air after the party and would be back in half an hour:
I was to go to bed. It wasn't until after one that he returned
—he'd taken the car with him and I heard him draw up
outside. I took it for granted what he'd been up to and
didn't bother even to ask. The next evening, of course, I
discovered I'd been wrong and things were far worse than
I'd suspected.'

One aspect of the case probably having no bearing on the
crime itself had mystified Arvo, though with Eeva's analysis
in mind, he was beginning to understand. 'But surely even
for a past-master in the outrageous, this was going to extremes: opera singers may be attracted by the melodramatic
and they're known to use pretty shady means to dispose of
rivals, but chloroforming, binding, gagging and abandoning
them indefinitely in remote country barns is stretching it a
bit. The singing of the part on just this one occasion must
have been of overwhelming importance to him. Have you
any idea why?'

'Somehow it was vital. Some time back we were in Oulu:
he was filling in for someone in a concert. He'd been drinking
heavily for months and was physically ill, probably as a
result. He'd got no future and he knew it and he didn't
much care, or so it seemed. Then he heard that the original
choice for the part of Don Giovanni in the Festival was in
trouble with the police and there was only the second choice,
the understudy, available. Maybe another stand-by would

be selected but that would take time. He changed literally
overnight: singing that part had become the whole purpose
of his existence. He gave up alcohol completely and did
everything possible to create the impression of a total refor-
mation. He even treated me as a human being. And when I
started rehearsing at Savonlinna he came with me, followed
minutely all that went on at rehearsals, persuaded Andrei to
let him take part occasionally, practised the rôle incessantly
when we were free and made sure it was taken for granted
that he was the accepted deputy. Of course nobody actually
imagined he'd be called upon. He got me to give him the
money for a made-to-measure costume and got it approved.
In fact everybody was a bit sorry for him.'

'That's still not an explanation.'

'I don't know myself exactly, though I'm sure it's connected largely with what I've told you already. He identified
himself with the character. And he was superstitious naturally, as that type often is, without admitting it openly. If
he could take over the part it would mean that luck was
with him, the fearless gambler: he'd be on his way to
re-establishing himself, to rising to even greater glory than
before. But there was something else too. You've probably
been told about his headaches, which were getting worse.
Something to do with his lifestyle perhaps but they frightened him, so much so that he was scared he was going to
die—he swung between heights of optimism and depths
of depression. And somehow by singing the part he was
challenging destiny, life, the devil himself, almost as if he
knew there'd be nothing beyond it. Are you absolutely sure
it wasn't suicide?'

'Not unless he devised a means of killing himself before
he entered the water. After such a long immersion the
autopsy can't be certain, though strangulation seems
ninety-eight per cent sure and there's no remaining evidence
of poison.'

'And I suppose no real idea of the time?'

'From the body itself, no. It could have happened days later. But it was that evening that he disappeared. From what we've heard he was never seen again after his dramatic disappearance, carried away by devils. From what you've been saying he wasn't likely to have missed the curtain call, unless something serious stopped him.'

'You've probably heard that Ilmari was the last known person to see him alive or at least hear him when he'd gone off towards the Suvorov Courtyard, saying he'd be back in time for the curtain call but he wanted a moment to himself. And then when Ilmari went to find him a moment or two after, he'd disappeared. Couldn't it have happened then?'

'If it was suicide, yes. If this had been a drama, it would have been the perfect moment, at least if your analysis of his behaviour is correct and it sounds feasible. But medical facts are against it. And Ilmari could be the murderer, who was naturally the last person to see the victim alive. Certainly he was never seen after that so far as is known. We know there's a lack of motive for Ilmari or can you suggest any possibility: rivalry, jealousy, resentment? In our short acquaintance I haven't got the impression of a murderer but you've known him longer and so can judge better.'

'Ilmari? Oh no, never. He'd have no motive and he's far too sane and sensitive. Maybe he's a bit detached: he's more interested in life itself than in the affairs of individuals, but he's uncomplicated and infinitely kind.'

'The antithesis of a Don Giovanni?'

'No. Both in their own ways could have enormous charm, though Peik's was more contrived.'

Arvo began to wonder how he had been analysed by his former fiancée and what the present verdict might be. However, policemen have more practical jobs to do.

'Let's go back in time,' he suggested. 'With no aspersions, can we start with you, only because you happen to be here.

You must have been on stage until the final curtain. What happened after?'

'I changed as quickly as I could. Surely you don't think I went off in my costume, murdered my husband and pushed him into the water, and then returned to change? Kaarina Laufach, our Elvira, who's a good kind soul, had heard during the interval about my decision and offered me a temporary home. Her husband was waiting for her and we went off together.'

'Were you alone at any time?'

'Oh Arvo, I can't remember now: it's far too long ago. I know I was so furious with Peik I didn't worry in the least about his disappearance. But that doesn't mean I murdered him. I'm not in the least a violent person.'

A tantalizing flicker of memory spotlighted a teenage Eeva attacking him with fists, nails and well-placed kicks on the shin: something about having been seen in a café-bar in apparently intimate conversation with the class glamour-queen. It hadn't quite come to murder, though. He grinned and shook his head.

'And if you're remembering your disgraceful goings-on with Salme Salonen—yes, I still haven't forgotten—you fully deserved what you got,' Eeva informed him tartly, reading his mind.

'We'll pass over your predisposition for murder,' he observed tolerantly. 'Can you recall the movements of your fellow singers?'

'I haven't the slightest idea, nor of Andrei's. And if you're thinking of Risto, you can forget it. He'd have been the last possibility. He knew I meant what I said: that I was leaving for good. So he had no conceivable reason.'

'Peik's attack on you must have upset him quite a lot, surely.' He was aware of Eeva's horrified gasp. 'Oh yes, I've heard about that. Motive enough to a deeply-sensitive withdrawn and devoted champion of his adored lady— Risto could well be a dragon-slayer, I think.'

'He's far too sensitive and gentle.'

'Superficially—but it's you who are the analyst. Have you ever turned your attention to Risto? He's intelligent, you know. And this isn't the first time you've decided to leave your unreliable, unstable husband, Donna Elvira in many ways as you are. Analyst, analyse yourself. Maybe he wanted to make sure this time. I wonder what dreams and hopes flourish in that sensitive mind?'

'I've never at any time encouraged him. In fact I've done my best to keep away from him.'

'I wonder why.' Arvo eyed her mockingly. 'Such a radical contrast to your wayward husband. Ottavio has more in him than meets the average person's eye, Eeva. Have you realized that?'

'Yes,' she said flatly, 'and it doesn't interest me. Do you think he's the only candidate?'

'Indeed, no. Though perhaps the most suitable—for you, that is. After all, I should be well-qualified to judge, having known you in your very infancy, so to speak.'

'And have absolutely no right to.' Eeva's attention had been drawn to the door behind her through which what appeared to be the captain of the vessel was pushing a loaded trolley. She turned back to say impatiently, 'Why on earth must men always be marrying women off? Don't you think I've had enough of the farce? Can't I at least mourn for one year more, as my Donna Anna was permitted? Because believe it or not, Arvo, I do mourn him. He was weak, wanton, callous and brash, but at the same time he had magic.'

The captain, splendid in a dazzle of gold braid, gleaming white and dashing navy blue, approached Eeva, bowed and kissed her hand. 'Madonna,' he cooed, with an Italianate gesture of the hand, 'I regret infinitely my discourteous absence until this late hour, but I have been concerned in preparing a delectable smörgåsbord which even you with all your experience of the haute cuisine of Europe may find interesting.' His eyes dwelt on Arvo, and he bowed again. 'Ah, the distinguished police superintendent from Helsinki. Keskinen, Maunu Keskinen. I am delighted to receive you on my yacht.'

'Really Maunu, you can't talk about receiving him now he's been on it for a couple of hours. Maunu is a very superior interior decorator and designer and he often turns his refined attention to stage designs. Did you see the recent *Fledermaus* production in Helsinki? The stage designs were all his own work. Much influenced in all sorts of ways by the Italians, as you can hear.'

More trolleys arrived and the group converged, selected, sampled and chatted to all and sundry. Eeva, and after her Risto, were drawn into the gossip and speculation, mainly concerned with the society whose photographs and activities normally provided materials for the glossies. Having filled and emptied his plate twice, Arvo strolled up to the sheet of glass that surrounded them and brooded over the unchanging panorama of lake, field and forest they were moving through, a world unchanged since the first Finns gradually made their way northwards some two thousand years before. After a moment he was joined by Risto.

'It's a strange affair in many ways,' Risto commented. 'There are so many parallels with the opera itself. Like reflections in water. The mirror image of the central character and his portrayer. The theme of revenge and retribution. You know he sang appallingly in the second act: I'm sure he must have been ill. And then when Nemesis in the form of the statue of a dead man called on him to repent and be saved, he yelled defiance, really holding the audience then with his performance. It was as if he was singing his own challenge to fate, his contempt for death, a recklessness based on utter despair. Sorry if that sounds over-dramatic but I think that everybody who heard him had the same feeling.'

'So you also would like it to be suicide?'

THE LAST OF THE SUMMER WINE

'Isn't that the only possible explanation?'

'You spoke just now of revenge. A short time before you'd seen him practically beat up his wife.'

'He slapped her face. Because she told him the truth. He's always been a self-centred callous brute but that evening he seemed to have gone berserk, lost every touch with reality. Each of us who was there, with the exception of Andrei and Ilmari Karhu, was ready to take some kind of action and I'm quite prepared to admit, I volunteered to carry it out.' Risto paused, looking down at his hands sheepishly.

'But you didn't?' Arvo was asking a question and the answer was hesitant.

'I'm afraid I didn't and I'm ashamed of my weakness. Like Hamlet, I lacked the necessary resolution.'

'Of course you didn't do it.' Eeva had joined them and put an arm round him in a motherly gesture. 'Risto wouldn't hurt a fly.'

He shook himself free with slight impatience. 'Peik wasn't a fly, though he might have been a tarantula or a particularly vicious cobra ready to strike to kill. I wouldn't hesitate to kill a snake or other animal. I wasn't afraid of the danger or even of the consequences. But the murder of another human being is something abnormal and sickening. It's a horrifying thing to defy the fifth commandment and the age-long ban on individual murder, whatever men do in battle. But in cold blood, without passion or fear, only a psychopath, a maniac, a savage or maybe a saint would be able to ignore or take on the momentous responsibility for murder. And I'm not any of those.'

He turned away abruptly and approached a trolley where coffee, fruit and pastries had replaced the delicacies of the smörgåsbord. The other four guests had gathered there and drew him and Eeva back into their circle. Eeva looked back questioningly at Arvo but he smiled, shook his head and lowered himself into a cushioned seat. He wanted to drift peacefully in a world of water and forest, to browse, possibly doze and let his subconscious mind sort through and shape into intelligible form the many impressions he had been receiving. The boat was moving quietly and smoothly within a green and golden bubble of light and colour where the lake shores had momentarily drawn together; the sun was no longer visible, only the rich glow of sunlit birches on the nearer bank. Here and there in the patch of sky above the trees, birds were congregating and making practice flights in preparation for their long journeys ahead. In places where the forest retreated, hay in stacks still dotted some of the sun-green meadows emerging from the water.

The saloon was a place of dream, of slanting light and darting reflections flashing across the glossy ceiling. When the shore receded again to the west, he noticed purple storm clouds banking up rapidly on the horizon, their menace intensified by the untouched radiance around them. As the clouds surged forward, swallowing up the sun, the gleam of the as yet unshadowed birch trees darkened instantaneously; now they smouldered luridly against the funeral green of the conifers. The forest was on fire, a fire without smoke or sound, but one that would burn away the very colour that was producing it, leaving skeleton limbs to be clothed by snow and ice. Colourless themselves they would transform the sunlight into rainbows against a background of unearthly blue. But first the rising wind that was driving the clouds must strip those branches and already the first heavy drops were spattering on them, loosening the hold of the tenuously clinging leaves, leaving the wind to detach, lift, whirl and deposit them in their floating millions on the lake waters.

The wines served with the meal had temporarily loosened tongues and now their bountiful host was bringing brandy, whisky and liqueurs to offer in the most exquisite Iittala glasses. Wine always made Arvo sleepy and the brandy accelerated the process. The raindrops that covered the windows obscured the water below, the sky above and the

endless encircling forest, and the boat began to rock gently
on opposing waves. His eyelids drooped and like most of
his now-silent somnolent companions, he drifted into a
half-familiar dream world. He was being led round a castle
battlement by a guide uncommonly like his school history
teacher who had no idea of the way and was continually
confronting locked doors and non-existent staircases, and
the sky was getting darker all the time. And he could hear
the teacher screaming, 'I've lost the paper, the plan I had
and winter's coming. Find it. Find it.' He jerked himself
awake, opening his eyes to survey his surroundings with
bewilderment and found one hand in his jacket pocket
clutching an envelope. He drew it out and blinked at it,
extracting automatically the letter it contained and starting
to read:

Arvo,
    I've just picked up what may be an interesting piece of
information for you . . .

Of course, the note he'd been reading when the phone
rang and he'd stuffed into his pocket and forgotten. He
read on:

According to reports, you're working on the Savonlinna
case, so I'm passing it on for what it's worth. I got it from
one of the Press Attachés at the Soviet Embassy that I
occasionally have a drink with. He'd had more than one
vodka and we were talking about Savonlinna which he'd
visited once.
    That Russian director they had there, Andrei Pavlov,
had the usual 'comrade' supplied to keep an eye on him
and apparently after the producer's unforeseen departure
westwards, poor 'comrade' who swears he'd been doped
—who knows?—was really in the dog-house and was sent
home for a salutary lesson after neglecting to take proper

care of his precious charge. Apparently he was a bit peeved about this and before departure let slip something that could be right up your street.

Naturally, where Mary went, her little lamb was bound to go and accordingly while Mary (or Andy if you prefer) was busy at the theatre, little lamb was near enough to join him without delay when he left. On a nice summer evening the battlements were a pleasant enough place and had the advantage of a good view over the bridge so that he could race after Andy if he happened to forget him. That night he'd wandered about half way in the direction of the Suvorov Courtyard when he thought he heard a splash from there. So he hurried along to see what it was—he would still have seen the bridge though he was getting a bit far away from it. Not that he noticed anything particularly startling: a man quite alone standing on the edge of the channel that runs through there, looking hard into the water. It was already getting rather dark, as it would be in the third week in July, and what with the foliage on the trees in addition, he couldn't see very well, but he gave as clear a description of the man as he could.

Sorry I'm running out of paper and time too—they're just closing this bar—but I'll attach the details of time and appearance to this note. They're in English shorthand I'm afraid but you can probably work it out.

How much use of the information you can make I don't know as naturally you'll get no confirmation from the joint it came from.

Be seeing you,

                                        Jock

As Arvo well knew, Jock was a resident Scots newsman, connoisseur of whisky rather than vodka, his ears pinned well back and happy to offer and receive in return any disposable crumbs of information. In the dim light of the saloon, Arvo puzzled over the squiggles and curves which would have been difficult enough to decipher in his own language: fortunately Pitman's method had been introduced during a business-studies short course he had attended some years back in London. He scribbled some notes of his own on the back of the envelope before shoving it deep down into his pocket and sat back to contemplate things. So that must have been it! The most and the least obvious solution and absolutely impossible to prove.

His companions slumbered peacefully for another hour. He watched them coming to, blinking round the saloon with startled eyes, trying to get their bearings, eyeing smugly their unconscious acquaintances. The cloud and rain had brought premature darkness and they talked in whispers in the twilight, nobody venturing for some obscure reason to locate the light switches. It was the captain himself, looking a teeny bit dishevelled as if he also might unglamorously have indulged in forty winks in his private cabin, who turned on the concealed lighting together with a wide-screen television, before promising coffee very shortly.

Eeva rejoined Arvo and they revived past memories while Arvo produced photographs of his family and a firm invitation to visit them. Eeva responded with her own invitation to join them for dinner in a private room that had been booked in the most renowned restaurant in Lahti.

Arvo welcomed the invitation with reservations. 'I'd like to very much,' he said, 'but I must first make sure of a train that will get me to Helsinki at a reasonable time. The Chief Superintendent will be expecting me bright and early in the morning. He's spent the weekend fishing, and come to think of it, so have I in a way.'

'I wonder which of you will have been the most successful,' Eeva mused.

'Stop fishing yourself,' Arvo retorted. 'Anyhow, I'm having the harder job: I've got to make sure about my fish before hooking it and even then, getting it ashore and into the frying-pan won't be all that easy, if it can be done at all.'

'That sounds ominous for someone,' Eeva said thoughtfully. 'Can I know what species of fish it is?'

'Not now. It might put you off your dinner, especially if there's fish on the menu. I could do with some reindeer stew if they've got it.'

'We could always ask.'

'Talking of animals, fish and fowl, I noticed from that map of yours that we pass rather near friend Ilmari's village.'

'Of course. It's quite near Lahti. Do you think he'd join us for dinner?'

'Why not telephone him and ask? Incidentally, I went to see Iris Lawton while I was in Sweden.'

'Iris? Not another girlfriend? You do get around.'

'A teacher friend. We first met when she was teaching on a summer course in England. She'd already spent some time in Finland some years before so we had an interest in common. We invited her to our home on her next visit.'

'You don't mean to say you know about . . . ?'

Arvo cut in swiftly. 'I know about quite a lot of things but I don't always talk about them. Isn't Iris a friend of Ilmari's?'

'She certainly was but I haven't seen anyone from Savonlinna—apart from Risto of course—since the end of the Festival. I suppose you've encountered Ilmari in the course of your duties, shall we say.'

'I did happen to call on him just a few days ago. And we happened to discover we had a friend in common. Tell him I met her in Sweden.'

'He'll come, even if he has to grow wings and fly there.' Could there have been a slight tinge of envy in Eeva's voice?

On its arrival in Lahti the cabin cruiser was moored among a few remaining yachts, rowing-boats and other craft. While the captain (now in a slightly less conspicuous suit) and his taciturn assistant were ensuring that all was shipshape, Eeva went to telephone and returned looking pleased. 'I was right,' she informed Arvo. 'It was rather amusing. He started off with a string of polite excuses till I told him about Iris. At that point I changed tack: of course I understood: I realized how busy he was: another time. And he had to reverse course even more abruptly: after all, he couldn't miss such a pleasant opportunity of meeting old friends—me and Risto that's to say, you're hardly an old friend—so he must allow himself to be persuaded.'

7. SELECTION FROM THE MENU

The captain and his crew were to be thanked with a complimentary dinner and eventually three taxis arrived to take everybody to the restaurant. The rain had eased off but overhead lighting, car and bus headlights and shop window illuminations dazzled in the mirror-wet road surfaces. Despite the drizzle, Lahti was very much alive on this early October Sunday evening with crowds of window-shoppers, strolling couples and families returning from visits to aunts and grandparents.

The party was escorted through a crowded restaurant to a quiet and pleasant room upstairs with a carnation-decked table laid for ten, Eeva having made a second telephone call to arrange for the two extra guests. The men being in the majority, the interior-designer captain as guest of honour headed the table with his assistant on his right, while Arvo as second guest of honour faced his from the foot of the table with Eeva on his right and an empty place for Ilmari on his left. As he looked along the two rows of chattering people, Arvo was aware as often before of one of the social drawbacks to a police career: apart from close friends, people tend to draw away from one, however blameless their lives. There is always a slight reserve, a hesitation to let their hair down and feel at ease. For Eeva, however, he would always remain the teenage boyfriend—could it have been that mentally-defective Salme Salonen who had saved him from the fate of spending the rest of his life being referred to as the magnificent Miss Eeva Ruuskanen's husband?

Ilmari arrived almost unnoticed among the general hilarity following the first cocktail and after introductions and handshakings, took his seat beside Arvo. He appeared serene and happy to be there but the probing eye on his right detected marks of strain and weariness round eyes and mouth.

'A busy day?' Arvo asked.

'Rather, yes. There's been a lot of foot trouble and various other problems resulting from that long spell of wet weather. And my partner's been off for the weekend. I've had to arrange for a telephone-sitter who's got this number in case of emergency.'

'Bad as being a policeman,' Arvo commented.

A swift smile of accord that flickered across lips and startlingly blue eyes faded into polite attention. 'You were in Stockholm on Friday as you'd arranged?' he asked.

'Yes. I called in on the Pavlovs in their very comfortable flat. They seem to be settling down well enough. I found them very interesting to talk to.' Arvo directed a meaningful look at Ilmari who merely continued to show polite interest. One forgets he's an actor, Arvo was thinking, though grand opera doesn't normally demand so much subtlety.

'It's Natasha who's having problems surely,' Ilmari suggested. 'Adapting herself to the standards of the decadent West won't come easy to her. Or is she dazzled by all the magnificence?'

'Problems indeed. She's been highly efficiently indoctrinated and she's loyal and it's only too easy to find the faults in our society without looking particularly hard for them. But they're a devoted couple and she's obviously much happier in Sweden with him than in Petroskoi without him.

'By the way,' Arvo continued, 'I've also been discovering what a bad memory you seem to have, even of really quite striking occurrences. Achieving one's ends by blackmail, for example.'

The corners of Ilmari's eyes lifted a fraction in slightly mocking concern. 'Really,' he drawled, 'a case of advanced amnesia, indeed.'

'I'd have assumed you'd be a law-abiding citizen anxious to help the police in every way.'

'So would I,' Ilmari murmured. 'What helpful information could I have held back?'

'As I've said, the use of blackmail.'

'Tell me more.'

'Peik Arvika's blackmailing of Dr Pavlov. And stop stalling.' Definitely the policeman taking over from the fellow guest.

'And how would a knowledge of that have been helpful?'

'As motive for a murder?'

'Not in the least. You'll have heard that Andrei met the demand in full and the chances of Peik's taking the matter further were far slimmer than the risk to Andrei of committing murder in an alien land. And I assure you on my honour that Andrei wasn't enraged: he'd got far too many other things on his plate to go round exacting retribution.'

Behind Ilmari an invisible waiter had been hovering with a large glossy menu: with the naturalist's sensitivity to unseen presences, Ilmari turned, took the menu and handed it to Arvo. 'They make an excellent reindeer stew here,' he recommended. Main course orders were taken and almost at once various dishes of hors d'oeuvre accompanied by schnapps appeared on the table. Eeva's attention was concentrated on increasingly vivacious neighbours while Arvo and Ilmari sat in silence, each absorbed in his own thoughts.

It was Eeva who finally took the conversation a stage further by turning to them shortly before the arrival of the main course.

'Didn't you say you'd visited Iris in . . . wherever she is now?' she asked Arvo. 'Or have you already talked about that?'

Ilmari acknowledged the mention of a common acquaintance with a slight lifting of the eyebrows. 'She's in Orrefors,' Arvo informed his questioner. 'She's teaching English in a glass factory there.' He glanced at Ilmari. 'I gave her your regards. She seemed a trifle put out at having heard nothing from you. I did my best for you by saying you probably hadn't got her address and anyhow had had big problems with your house.' Recent speculations had suggested a possible explanation for this particular riddle, if riddle it was and not merely a natural development, and he scanned Ilmari's face with apparent casualness. It showed only gentle concern.

'Does she seem happy there?' he asked. 'That's the main thing, isn't it?'

'Iris has an infinite interest in life, particularly in new surroundings. She seemed very happy.'

Ilmari nodded gravely as if he had expected this. 'She wasn't unhappy in Finland, you know. I think she felt very much at home here. Unfortunately she probably thought that a change of country might be advisable.'

With arrival of his steaming reindeer stew imminent, Arvo analysed this particular manifestation of assumed indifference. He surveyed the aromatic concoction before him with absorbed appreciation, suddenly lifting his eyes to meet Ilmari's and glimpsing for an unguarded second a misery so complete that he was moved to pity.

Arvo offered wine to his two companions before filling his own glass. 'Of course it isn't my business,' he observed, 'but surely it's not difficult for a Finn to spend a few days in Sweden looking around.'

There was a suggestion of hard control in Ilmari's reply, but he spoke even more serenely. 'Yes, indeed. As soon as things slacken down a bit, I'll definitely be looking her up.

Did you gather she'd been much shocked by the murder?'

'She hadn't even heard about it: I was the first to tell her. Even then she was so unprepared that she thought I was joking.'

'Unprepared?'

'Murders aren't all that common after all, especially among acquaintances, however unpopular they may be. She didn't shed any tears for Peik Arvika, though whether she would have congratulated his murderer I've no idea.'

Ilmari was uneasily examining the as yet untasted fish he had ordered, almost as if he expected it to rear up and make some accusation. 'You're wondering what to make of my apparent loss of interest in Iris,' he said slowly. 'In fact you quite rightly don't believe a word of it. But I've got a motive for the murder that may not have occurred to you.'

'A selfish one?'

'If a very deep feeling for another person can be construed as a selfish motive, yes. Did Iris tell you about our conversation at Koli?'

'That Peik overheard? Yes.'

'Isn't there an overwhelming motive for murder there?'

'I'm sorry. I'm not with you.'

'I think you are. That final night Peik was insane enough to have extended his blackmail tactics. He knew Iris was in Viipuri and he knew exactly why. How easy and commendable of him to pass on all relevant information to the proper authorities, including of course her easily-proved residence in Savonlinna and acquaintance with Natasha's husband.'

For a moment Arvo's fork spearing a lump of succulent meat paused in mid-air while he contemplated it. Why, he wondered, should Ilmari be exposing himself to suspicion and was he aware of a slight flaw in the motive he was admitting to?

'What would Arvika have hoped to gain by blackmailing you?' he inquired. 'You were without influence and so long as Eeva remained with him, he was adequately supplied with money. And I don't suppose you're a particularly rich man anyhow.'

'I suppose I've got enough money put by to last him some time: after all, I'd heard his wife's decision to leave him. And as I've explained, Peik was very far from normal that evening: in fact he was lashing out in all directions.'

'It's possible, yes,' Arvo admitted. 'Though I don't quite see the connection with your breaking off relations with Iris. Did he blackmail you?'

'No, to your question. As to your remark, there are plenty of journals in this country which specialize in serving up scandal at the coffee table. Any hint of a connection between a certain Miss Lawton allegedly on her first visit to Finland and recent associates of a couple of Russian defectors might well set the moles burrowing, if that's the right metaphor here.'

Eeva had been following the conversation for some time without making any comment. Now she broke in. 'That's one virtue of the Communist East,' she declared. 'However extraordinary the versions of the truth they present, they don't encourage that kind of perversion. Much of the un-savoury reputation that Peik enjoyed was the result of their exaggerations and innuendoes. He'd often lead them on, of course, blackening his own image out of a kind of contempt. We were divorced at least a dozen times. And now there's the gloating over me, everything a hair's breadth the safe side of libel naturally, photos of me from archives at various receptions and parties talking to different stage personalities, Peik being invisible or somewhere in the distant background with the clear implication that this or that one might have been involved in the murder.'

She laid down her knife and fork and pushed her plate back, turning her head to face Arvo squarely. 'Why must all this continue?' she demanded. 'An unwanted human being is dead and we're still not sure it wasn't suicide. If anyone killed him, he had ample justification. Why must we keep raking over the ashes, causing distress to so many people who should have been feeling only relief?'

'Because we live in a community and wherever human beings live together there must be sanctions, the strongest of them against murder. Would you be happy to associate in friendship with someone who you knew had taken your husband's life, whatever his reasons, except possibly immediate protection from violence against himself or another?' Arvo had argued about this before and would doubtless do so again but he still took the matter with intense seriousness, staring unseeingly down the table at the interior designer/cabin-cruiser captain at the other end, who cringed and looked down quickly at his plate, as if discovered committing some appalling misdemeanour.

Nothing could have dried up a conversation more effectively. After an awkward silence, Eeva turned to address a remark to the man beyond her and was drawn into the middle-of-the-table discussion.

Arvo glanced at his watch and discovered he would have to leave in little more than five minutes. He turned to Ilmari who seemed to be deep in thought.

'I'd very much appreciate your help,' he began. 'You've almost certainly gathered I've been engaged in clutching at straws this evening, considering every last possibility that might disprove the firm conclusion I've reached in this case. I wish I could disprove it but nothing helps. I'll discuss it in conference tomorrow morning at headquarters but I know I'm going to get general agreement. I know who Arvika's murderer is without any doubt at all.'

Ilmari said nothing, waiting for an explanation.

Arvo took out the envelope and unfolded the papers inside, exposing the near-incomprehensible shorthand. 'I was given this by an absolutely reliable authority who got hold of the information it sets out direct from the Soviet Embassy. Originally this information was supplied by a certain Stanislav, who acted as guide and companion to Dr

Pavlov while he was in Savonlinna. It seems this gentleman was waiting for the doctor on the battlements at the final performance and apparently only just missed witnessing the murder. He has given a description of someone who must almost certainly have been the murderer himself.'

Again Arvo paused but got no response.

'This description makes it one hundred per cent sure that it was Dr Andrei Pavlov who murdered Peik Arvika.' There was a horrified gasp from Ilmari, who started to speak but was silenced when Arvo continued what he had to say.

'This will inevitably be not only an extremely serious charge to make but will involve complications of extreme complexity. We must first of course issue a warrant which will have to be passed on to the Foreign Office, who will then have to apply to the Swedish Government for the extradition of the accused man. It's possible that this will be met with a refusal, though I doubt it in a case of murder.' Again Ilmari tried to intervene and was silenced. 'If Dr Pavlov is returned to this country, there may well be an application from the Soviet authorities for his return to his native country.'

'It's impossible,' Ilmari almost shouted. Arvo silenced him by saying, 'If I'm going to catch my train, I must be out of this room in two minutes and no more. The question that will concern you is what will happen to Natasha. She may decide to accompany her husband with the risk of being returned to her own country as an illegal immigrant. Now you're an intelligent, experienced and sensitive person. You speak Russian: you are partly Russian. You know both Dr Pavlov and Natasha already. Nothing can be done for two or three days officially, though unofficially we shall inform the Swedish authorities probably tomorrow and ask if a discreet watch can be kept on the Pavlovs. Immediately they're informed of the possibility of extradition, it would be a humane action on your part to go to Stockholm to be at their side to advise them, particularly Natasha, as you

think best. By then we ourselves should have more information about the exact position and will supply you with
it. Otherwise you may have to rely on your own judgment,
with the realization naturally that any kind of escape will
be absolutely impossible.' He glanced again at his watch
and gasped. 'Look here,' he said, 'I'll have to fly. Can you
give me a lift to the station in your car. Though there won't
be time for further discussion, I'm afraid.'

He rose and apologized abjectly but swiftly to the
company. 'I'm terribly sorry I've only just noticed the time
and I've got about five minutes to catch my train. Can I
thank you profusely for your wonderful kindness without
the individual goodbyes I'd so much have preferred to give?'
He bent down to assure an astonished Eeva that his wife
would be phoning the following day to invite her to dinner
so he would soon be seeing her again, and sped down the
staircase with Ilmari close at his heels, each experiencing the
guilty feelings of two unfortunate diners who had suddenly
realized their complete inability to pay the bill. Five minutes
later as he collapsed into the last coach of the departing
train, Arvo chuckled over the astonished face of the interior-
designer who had been chattering while Arvo's announcement was being made and had been staggered at the frantic
break for freedom of the august majesty of the law.

8. WINTER WIND

In Helsinki the following Thursday brought a foretaste of
winter rigours ahead. From the normally placid Gulf of
Finland a knife-edge gale scraped up surging wave-crests.
In town streets it pierced through inadequate autumn coats
to freeze the very bone-marrow within, grazed collar-
shielded cheeks and noses and forced teardrops from smart-
ing eyes. The sluggish damp chill of Helsinki was swept up

and concentrated into a weapon of cruel efficiency.

Immediately he emerged from his car Arvo was shrivelled by the blast that met him. With fur hat over his ears and scarf covering his chin, he raced for police headquarters to bask in the warmth that embraced him as soon as the heavy outer door closed behind him. Having shed his protective cocoon inside his office, he was immediately alerted by telephone to the fact that a Mr Ilmari Karhu had just arrived to see him. He telephoned to the desk sergeant below asking for Mr Karhu to be sent up.

Ilmari looked ill at ease, though whether because he hadn't had enough time to thaw out after his journey to headquarters or for some other reason remained to be seen. Familiar as he was with the haunts of wild life, he was clearly unaccustomed to encountering a member of the police force in his natural habitat. His greeting was reserved and there was an unusual rigidity about him as he sat down on the chair indicated.

He hesitated before speaking almost as if, having carefully rehearsed his words, they had evaded him at the last minute. The marks of tension in his face had deepened during the past few days: there was a tightening of eye and cheek muscles: a withdrawn suffering look that had replaced the serenity still apparent a few days before.

Small talk might relieve something of the tension, so inevitably Arvo resorted to climatic conditions. 'I suppose the weather's still quite bearable in Lahti,' he commented, 'or have you been in Helsinki for some time?'

Aware of the kindness that prompted the remark, Ilmari relaxed slightly and with a brief smile observed, 'No, I caught an early train this morning and met with a chilly reception at the station here. I'd forgotten that living near the sea has its drawbacks as well as its summer pleasures.' Again he paused and the words that followed were abnormally pedantic as if he were addressing a police court rather than a recent dinner companion. 'Having in mind what you confided to me a few days ago about your intentions relating to the Pavlovs, or rather to Andrei, and your request for my assistance, I was wondering whether you had taken any further steps in the matter.'

The delivery of this ponderous request, as stilted as its content, proved infectious and Arvo found himself responding in kind.

'I have to express my regret that such action has indeed been necessary,' he replied. 'The matter in question has been submitted to the Ministry of Foreign Affairs who will have the onus of applying for the extradition of Dr Pavlov from his present place of residence in order to answer the charges against him.'

'And his wife?'

'She would naturally in no way be involved in the matter, the more especially as there would be no question of her appearing as a witness.'

'Will he stand trial here or be returned to his own country?'

'Here, naturally. And if he's found guilty, his sentence will be served here.'

'And after that? Extradition to his own country to face the penalty for escape?'

Arvo avoided committing himself. 'I'm afraid that's not my province,' he replied.

Leaning forward with his forearms on his knees, Ilmari meditated for a moment in silence. Then he straightened, almost as if in relief at having shed a burden.

'I'd hoped the need for this wouldn't arise,' he said more rapidly and more naturally. 'I've put so much into my practice and it's useful, creative, humanitarian work—relieving just a bit of the suffering and pain that being alive entails: there's so much unhappiness and pain among people and animals. Nobody will have suffered on account of the death of Peik Arvika and in some ways perhaps the world's a better place. That was one of the reasons I killed him. He was like a horrible growth that could only cause more suffering if it wasn't removed. You know, I've sometimes wondered about some of those two thousand women that Don Giovanni himself betrayed: what would have been the future for some of them? Nobody seems to think about that. Peik shared to the full his utter indifference to other people's needs and feelings. And I realized during the performance that night he'd developed a meanness all his own: he could be spiteful. He'd believe Andrei would turn on him as soon as he'd got to safety, so the chances were he'd carry out his threat of exposure as soon as the performance ended. Consequently I was forced to remove him when I did.'

'How did you kill him?'

'I strangled him from behind: it's not difficult for someone with a professional knowledge of anatomy. It was easy enough to push the body into the channel: the difficulty was to keep it from rising to the surface. I knew of the grille and realized that if the body were to be stuck under there the lower prongs would hold it. So I forced it under.'

'How? Nobody has reported that you or your clothes were wet in any way.'

'As the Commendatore I carried a sword. Only a stage property of course, but it served the purpose of moving . . .' Ilmari sank his head on his hands, appalled by the vividness of the remembered scene.

'When did you actually do this?'

Ilmari appeared not to have heard him, only looking up vaguely when he realized silence had fallen. 'I beg your pardon?' he repeated.

Arvo repeated the question.

'Immediately after our exit,' Ilmari said. 'It was the only possible time. I knew that five minutes would barely serve so I concentrated everything on getting it right. I really didn't enjoy it, you know.'

The understatement of the century, Arvo reflected, when one considered the sensitivity of the man involved. Ilmari was speaking again. 'I'm not trying to excuse myself, but there was another reason. Those headaches he had. For some time I'd suspected a brain tumour. That would probably have accounted also for some features of his behaviour. I'd mentioned it a day or two before to Dr Turunen and he told me in confidence that Peik had been to him a short time before without telling anyone else. He'd suspected it himself and so far as he could tell without surgical tests, so did the doctor. He'd urged an operation but Peik had put him off. I think he believed he was going to die and that was why the Don Giovanni part had become so important to him. It isn't quite impossible he would have killed himself, though I don't know if he was that kind of person. But in either case, it was essential for him to die, whether for the sake of others for for his own sake. It was an appalling task that I had to make myself do, and I'm still living with it.'

'If it was so altruistic, why didn't you report it at once?'

'Was it altruistic? It just seemed something that had to be done. Surely it's only natural to avoid punishment if you can? I suppose I'll be in prison some years but I'll come out to my own country a free man. And after all, I am guilty. I've been spending the past few days arranging for a young vet to take over my practice for a few years to gain experience: I told my partner the truth yesterday evening. He'll give all the help and advice he can to the newcomer: he's one of my best friends, a really good man.

'The world will know about it soon, I suppose,' he continued. 'The sort of thing that makes the headlines, isn't it? "The Opera Case: the motiveless murder where melodrama becomes reality." "Retribution for Finnish Don Giovanni—" how he would have hated that description! Large fees will be offered for my story of how and why I murdered him.' Ilmari, the serene and tolerant, gave a snort of contempt and repugnance. 'For the intellectual, an object of psychological and social analysis. Was I in fact motivated by feelings of inhibited envy, inadequacy or possibly the arrogance of moral superiority?' He crossed to the window and stood for a moment watching the depersonalized figures below, some challenging, others cringing before the shrivelling force of the wind.

Arvo remained silent, noticing how by degrees the tension passed out of him, to be replaced whether by some natural process or by rigid self-mastery he couldn't guess, by the old tranquillity.

When he turned towards Arvo again, Ilmari spoke gently: 'I suppose you'll need my statement now.'

'In a moment, yes. First I'm going to tread on forbidden ground. Has this been why you've avoided all contact with Iris?'

There was a long interval of silence, in which Ilmari stood looking at the desk in front of him, his face and eyes empty of all expression, while Arvo cursed himself for unpardonable clumsiness. But it was with the old quiet smile that Ilmari answered: 'You know her too. Could you have sought her friendship, talked to her, or even written to her, seeing yourself as what you are, a murderer?'

'I think you could have told her perhaps, in a letter if you couldn't face her with the story.'

'How could she have reacted? How would your own wife react? And Iris isn't in love with me, you know. Could you ever consider meeting her with that between you? These hands, they've crushed out a man's life, and even with all the understanding and affection in the world between you, she wouldn't be able to escape the awareness of that moment.'

'That's true, on one level. But we live at so many levels at the same time and at all those other levels she'll accept and understand, I think. And time will do its own work.'

Ilmari shook his head. 'She can't be, mustn't be, in any way involved in this. That was the real penalty I knew I had to face when I made the decision. Perhaps if we'd been closer . . . As it is, she'll be a little shocked when the news breaks, bewildered and rather thankful. If you don't mind, we won't talk about it any more. Shall we get on with the statement?'

The trial attracted all the publicity that could have been expected though the accused seemed unaware of it, responding to the long series of interrogations with passive acquiescence, receiving sometimes the over-effusive sympathy of friends and acquaintances with polite detachment, retreating into a secluded world of his own which protected him reasonably well from all but his own personal unhappiness. Brought to trial, he was rightly harangued about taking the law into his own hands, the arrogance of the individual who puts himself above accepted moral conventions, however urgent the situation. The circumstances surrounding the murderer's blackmail were played down by both prosecution and defence; there was little question of the defendant's guilt and the prosecution put up no determined opposition to the defence lawyer's plea for mercy. In the circumstances, the sentence was a light one: four years' imprisonment (with a reduction to two years for good behaviour tacitly understood). Some of his friends had a strong impression that the prisoner would have preferred a longer term: prison for him might be a form of refuge, an ideal environment for his own unhappiness.

The dull numbness of despair was not to last long.

Two weeks after he had taken up his new quarters, the first of Iris's letters arrived: short, cheerful and about nothing much in particular.